SO THIS WAS ENGLAND

by

Christina Reis

kate-obrien.co.uk

First edition published by Silver Quill Publishing 2022

www.christinareis.co.uk

ISBN: 978-1-912513-39-0

UK spelling observed

Typeset in Georgia

Silver Quill Publishing

www.silverquillpublishing.com

Dedicated to...
My children, who always believed in me.

Chapter One

Manchester 2009

It had been a long, long, journey; brief in time, but immense in miles, conflicting emotions and culture. Just getting on a plane had changed her life irreversibly. Yesterday morning, a lifetime away, she was a different species: human, female, adult. Now she felt more like a yam or a plantain; alive, but with nothing else to say or be. She was crammed into a van with five other people. There were three seats along the sides and they sat facing each other. The van was so narrow it was difficult not to touch the knees of the person opposite and she shifted uncomfortably every few minutes.

The other passengers were a middle-aged Asian lady who smiled benignly every now and then, and four young men of various ethnic backgrounds. No one had a common language, so they were unable to converse. They had set off in daylight, though it was seven in the evening. The bright sky contrasted sharply with the bitterly cold air. She had been told that this was spring time in England. It was dark now. She was tired, but too uncomfortable to sleep. It was a relief to be able to stay silent, at least. The past two days, since she had stepped off the plane from Zimbabwe, had been one long interview after another. At least she was having a break from interrogation.

That morning she had been sitting in a corridor, waiting to be interviewed. The door next to her was slightly ajar, and she heard a woman's voice describing a man's entry into the country in the inside of a lorry's tanker. Apparently, he had been dragged out unconscious and was taken to hospital. The distortion of the woman's voice told her it was a speaker phone. A man began to say something in a language she did not recognise. At that point, the door was shut and she heard no more. She wondered idly if that man was one of her companions.

Suddenly, she realised that they were slowing down. The van turned a corner into a cobbled street of terraced houses. They stopped outside one door and the driver signalled to her to get out.

"You're the first one home," he said cheerfully, as he slammed the van door shut behind her.

"Number seven. You're in an HMO. House of multiple occupancy. Someone will be round tomorrow to tell you what's what. The other people are in. Look, the door's open."

She turned to face the house indicated. It was dark. There was smoke coming out into the night and raised voices competed with the beeping of a smoke alarm. Hesitantly, she peered into the doorway, then back at the van, but the driver was already backing out and in seconds had roared off into the darkness. Two pieces of charcoal were hurled onto the pavement.

"She's burnt the fucking toast again!" screamed a voice from within. A face appeared in the doorway, glaring angrily. She was young and pretty, with olive skin and jet black hair.

"Speak English?" the person demanded.

"Yes, I'm Mary, from Zimbabwe. I'm staying here for a few weeks, until my asylum claim is sorted. Then I'll send for my daughter."

"A few weeks! You'll be here for years. We're all waiting. Get used to it!"

With that, the girl flounced off inside and disappeared, leaving the front door open behind her.

Gingerly, Mary entered the house. The front door led straight into what seemed to be a lounge.

"Don't mind her." A voice, calm and gentle, came from another corner of the room. A tall, dark-skinned middle-aged woman was sitting at a table. "Welcome. I'm Giselle, from the Congo." She had a heavy African accent. "Tu parles francais?"

"No, sorry," Mary replied regretfully.

"My English is not good. Mitra's is much better. But she is very young and very – er –angry. The immigration officer said she was eighteen and an adult. He's never had a teenage daughter or sister. She is fourteen, I think."

It was the first normal conversation Mary had had since she started on her journey.

"Have you eaten?" Giselle asked.

Mary could not remember when she last ate, and did not feel hungry, but allowed Giselle to make her some tea and toast.

"Come on, I'll show you round the house. Your room's upstairs. Only Mitra sleeps downstairs."

Her room was small and bare, containing just a bed, a carpet and a cupboard. It was much more basic and sparse than she expected. But her possessions were few, and would easily fit in. She had only a carrier bag with a change of clothes and some photographs in it.

She put her things in the cupboard and lay down on the bed. It was surprisingly comfortable and she realised how tired she was. Soon, she fell asleep. In her dreams she was back at home, talking to her mother about work and they were laughing together, quietly at first, then louder and louder until the laughter turned to sobs. In the dream, Mary took her mother's hand to comfort her, but the hand felt soft and dry and she realised it was a pillow. She woke with a start, and for a moment she had no idea where she was. Then the last two days came flooding back to her; the long journey, the previous night in a detention centre, the endless van drive. The sobbing was real, muffled slightly by the thin wall between her and the next room. She didn't know who it was. The crying stopped after about half an hour, but Mary found it hard to sleep again. Tired though she was, when she closed her eyes her mother's face appeared before her; jubilant and elated in victory, determined and strong in defeat, caring and supportive with her followers, tranquil and relaxed in death at her hastily arranged funeral.

People told her that her mother was a heroine, and she must be so proud of her, and of course, she was. But sometimes, selfishly, she did not want a heroine. She just wished for an ordinary mother. She sat on her bed, waiting for morning. As the dawn was breaking, she peered out of the small window. The house was on a hill and rows upon rows of streets just like this one stretched out down towards a main road. In the distance, buses and cars passed occasionally along that road, too far away to be heard, and looking like small toys. Otherwise, the area was deserted until a young man came into view in a street at right angles to Mary's. He had long brown hair in a ponytail which protruded from the back of his baseball cap. He walked quickly, hands deep in the pockets of his jacket, broad shoulders hunched against the cold. She watched the pony tail until it was a mere speck.

"Well, Amia, what do I do now?" She realised she had said the words out loud. She knew the answer anyway. Her mother was a heroine and would want her to get on with it. "But I'm not my mother," she said aloud again.

Her mother had left her with a lot to live up to. She looked around her. She had a bed, a change of clothes, her precious photographs and a five-pound note given to her by the van driver to buy herself an evening meal. So this was England. She was cold, she was lonely and she was homesick.

But she was safe.

Chapter Two

At six o'clock, Mary ventured downstairs, nervously listening for sounds of the others' movements. A grey dawn was creeping over the sky. Through the window she could see there were lights in the windows opposite. In the gaps between their curtains she watched people getting dressed, preparing food, washing up. She envied them. They had lives to be getting on with. She sat on the sofa, staring into space, listening to the tick of the plastic clock on the wall.

After a while, she heard stirrings from the little downstairs bedroom, occupied by Mitra. Seconds later, Mitra stumbled into the kitchen area, dressed in oversized pyjamas and floppy slippers. Apart from her olive skin, jet black hair and eyes, she resembled every English teenager Mary had seen in films.

Without greeting Mary, Mitra got out a packet of cereal. She was already munching away when, as an afterthought, she shook the packet in Mary's direction.

"Oh, thanks," said Mary, even though she wasn't hungry. "That's kind of you."

A grunt was the only reply. After what seemed like a decade, but was actually a couple of hours, Giselle appeared and took Mary off to the local shop on the corner, as Mary had been given five pounds to spend on food by the van driver. She explained to Giselle that it was supposed to be for a meal yesterday, but she had no idea where the shops were. She bought some bread and some vegetables, but five pounds didn't go far.

When they returned, Mitra was still in pyjamas, slumped on the sofa, watching television. She didn't acknowledge either of them as they sat down beside her.

There was a loud knock on the door. Mitra groaned and flounced out of her seat.

"Don't break the fucking door down!" she growled as a young white man entered. He ignored her and looked across at Mary.

"You speak English?" Mary nodded. "I'm William. I'm the support worker for this area. How are you settling in?"

He had a half inch growth of brown hair on his previously shaved head, sticking straight up from his scalp like fur. He was confident, and almost unbearably cheerful, but he seemed friendly enough. Mary, tired as she was at being questioned and talked at, began to relax a little. He had a lap top and showed her a video about life in Britain, which gave her a break from listening to his voice.

Half an hour passed pleasantly enough until Mitra crossed the room and tripped over what looked to Mary like a bundle of clothes in the corner. There was a cry of protest from the bundle, and for the first time, Mary realised there was another person in the room, curled up with her knees bent underneath her and her forehead on the floor.

"Be more careful!" Giselle remonstrated in her strong African accent. "You could have hurt Hafida!"

"Oh, for god's sake! I thought she was a fucking carpet. Why has she got to be there, anyway? She's in the way."

"You know why, Mitra. She's doing penance. It's where she wants to be." William interrupted what may have turned into an argument. "Watch your language, Mitra. That's not a nice word in English. It's not good to talk like that."

"Why should I care? Does anyone care about me in this fucking country? Did anyone teach me this language? I learnt it at the youth club. They believe I'm fourteen. You don't. Do I get to go to school, like everyone else? No. Have I got parents to help me? No. My friends at the club go on school trips, learn things. What do I do? Nothing. Are you going to help me? No. Then fuck, fuck, fuck!!"

She retreated to her room, slamming the door so hard that it shook the fragile walls surrounding it. The heap on the floor that was Hafida shuddered slightly. Mary got up to go after Mitra, but William and Giselle remained unperturbed.

"Leave her to stew," William advised Mary.

Giselle agreed. "We get this at least once a week, sometimes once a day," she said resignedly.

"Well, can't something be done for her?" said Mary tentatively, aware of her status as a newcomer.

William was writing on a clipboard and didn't look up. "Not my problem. Immigration says she's eighteen and she's got no papers."

He finished writing and stood up. "Here's my number if you need anything. I'm only available in office hours, but there's a number to ring if there's an emergency outside those times. Please only use it in an emergency. Take this card to the post office to get your money, it's due every Wednesday. Giselle, show her where to go."

He was out of the door before Mary could ask what office hours were in this country, and what was considered an emergency. She looked at the card she'd been given. The photograph taken at the immigration centre was in one corner and there was a number, her name and a date of birth of the first of January. She had arrived with no passport in case the Zimbabwean authorities were on the lookout for her. Although she'd told the immigration authorities her real date of birth, somehow, it was discarded. It was so hard to hang on to her own identity in such a strange situation. But at least she was beginning to feel less fearful of capture.

Hafida got up. She was tall, painfully thin and looked about forty years old, a similar age to Mary.

"Hi, I'm Mary." She proffered a hand, but Hafida only pulled her clothes tightly around her. Her lips gave a polite smile, but her eyes were completely expressionless.

"She can't speak English," said Giselle. "Mitra translates for her as their languages are similar. Hafida's from Afghanistan, and speaks Dari and Mitra's own language is Farsi."

Hafida seemed unaware that she was being talked about. She walked away slowly, head bowed and silent.

"She's gone to her room. She doesn't leave the house much. We know nothing about her, really."

"What do people do round here? I was a teacher at home. I had my own work to go to and my mother was a political activist. I helped with her causes and looked after my daughter and my pupils. I've been told I'm not allowed to work."

"I know it's hard," said Giselle sympathetically. "But at least you're safe here."

"I'd do cleaning for someone, or any kind of stuff if they'd let me, but I'm not used to sitting around."

"We all feel like that at first. We try to find some purpose." Giselle was understanding and kind. "You'll have some money on Wednesday and there's a group I can take you to on Thursday. We learn to fill up the days. Also, they will send you for a medical. They want to make sure you're not bringing any diseases here."

It was all quite bewildering to Mary. She couldn't help feeling, despite what Mitra told her, that she wouldn't wait long for leave to remain. It seemed almost impossible to imagine years of this life without work.

"Oh, there's something else! William should have told you. We go to an immigration place every two weeks. You'll get a card to use as a bus ticket, but it's only useful for that one ride." Giselle smiled as she spoke. "I'd go with you but we'll probably have to go on different days. They need to see that we're still here."

This was more baffling than ever. Mary had nowhere to go and no money. Of course she would be here until she was told she could stay.

The house was too small to avoid the others and, unlike Africa, there was nowhere to sit outside. It was really cold, so the open air would be far from comfortable anyway. So they stayed, cooped up together in their little home.

Giselle showed her round, and made sure she knew where everything was in the kitchen. "I'll take you to the African shops tomorrow," she promised. "We get some money and usually take a trip there straight after. It's nice to have some familiar food."

This was something to look forward to, at least. The experience with the five pound note made her realise money didn't go far in this country. However, if she was not allowed to work, even shopping, albeit carefully, would take her mind off the horrific experiences which at the moment were so fresh and vivid.

Giselle was looking at her and seemed to read her mind, as she said, "Soon you will get used to your memories. We've all been there. We know how it feels."

Mary smiled, grateful for the understanding words without having to explain.

Next day they set off for the post office. That is, everyone except Hafida, who took up her usual position on her corner of the carpet. Mitra spoke to her in Farsi and she replied in monosyllables.

"What did she say?" asked Giselle as they left the house.

"Not coming, of course. She daren't go out until it's nearly closing time. She's frightened that she might get picked up.by immigration."

"How did you find all that out?" said Mary. "She hardly spoke one word."

"It's the same every Wednesday. I've heard it before, lots of times." Her tone was impatient, uncaring and as completely detached as only a schoolchild could be, and Mary wondered how anyone could believe that she was eighteen years old.

She stepped outside with the others. The whole world beyond their door appeared to be in black and white, or more accurately, shades of grey. It was raining, a fine drizzle that turned the pavements into dull, greasy slabs. Mary looked around at the houses they passed, all identical to theirs except for a different coloured door or occasionally a gold coloured letter box instead of a black one. Parked cars lined the route, obscuring the view of the traffic passing along the road, detectable only by the engine noises. Crossing the street was a perilous venture which the others achieved with ease.

They reached the post office. The queue was outside the door for several yards. The whole process took at least half an hour. The rain was beginning to soak through Mary's thin coat and soon she was shivering. She thought about her school at home and her pupils playing in the sunshine surrounded by fields. She could hear their shouts of laughter. How could she survive here? Although there were lots of people around, nobody spoke. Everyone just stood patiently waiting, not looking at each other. So different from the hustle and bustle generated by a crowd of people back home.

At last they were on their way to the food shop, but once there, another shock awaited Mary. The money she'd been given appeared quite adequate until she saw the prices of ordinary fruit and vegetables she would buy at home. Everything was at least five times more than the prices she was used to.

"It has to come a long way," Giselle told her. "That costs. But, also, these African shopkeepers know there's always a market, no matter how expensive. The only thing we can buy to connect us with home is the food."

That evening, Giselle cooked supper for them all. Hafida took hers to her room but the others sat around the table. It felt very strange to Mary to be eating with two women she hardly knew, but in a way it was comforting that they were in the same situation as she was. They were just more used to it. It occurred to Mary that she should offer to cook one evening, but somehow, she felt too tired and numb to suggest it. But the thought hung around in the back of her mind like a neglected task.

That night, she dreamed of her mother again and saw her laughing, crying, orating, celebrating victories, comforting her during her daughter Sara's birth. At dawn, she stood by the window, watching the young man with the ponytail as he walked down the street on his way to work. His arrival signalled the start of a new day. He was her only example, so far, of ordinary life in this strange country. Everything and everyone else was extraordinary.

Chapter Three

The next day, Giselle took Mary to a refugee social centre at a nearby church. It was good to get out and explore as it took her mind off her grief, but the streets looked so similar to her that she felt she would never find her way back. They entered a large room in one of several church buildings, unlike the single hall she worshipped in at home.

There were already a few people around. To her surprise, they all seemed to be from different countries to her own. For some reason, she'd expected that everyone would be at least from Africa. But Giselle explained that there were people from Iran, Iraq, Afghanistan, Pakistan, and China; and Romany families from Eastern Europe were there, as well as a few countries neighbouring her own. Religious differences didn't seem to be a problem and there were separate rooms off the main one to use as prayer rooms.

Giselle immediately found a group of friends from the Congo and introduced Mary, but after a minute or two, someone entered the room and grabbed Giselle by the arm and whisked her away, chattering loudly in Lingala. Giselle looked apologetically over her shoulder at Mary, who smiled reassuringly. However she felt more nervous and uncomfortable than she wanted to appear.

She glanced around the room, which was now beginning to fill up. There was a table with a pile of clothes and household goods in one corner and at the far end some people were gathered round a computer monitor apparently receiving instruction of some kind. A smell of fragrant spicy food came from an open door, through which there was a stream of people carrying cups of tea and biscuits. Summoning her courage, Mary approached the group by the computer.

"May I join you?" she asked hesitantly "This is my first visit. I'm not sure of the routine."

"Please come if you can speak such good English!" A white woman about her own age welcomed her in to the circle. "I could really do with some support! We're having a language lesson."

"Well, I taught English back in Zimbabwe. But my pupils were children and teenagers."

"You'll find this much easier, then. Everyone here wants to learn and you don't have to nag them to do their homework."

It was nice to feel wanted and Mary passed an enjoyable hour in the company of the teacher and pupils. Food was served at lunchtime, cooked by an Iraqi lady.

"Is that lady the chef here?" Mary asked the teacher.

"Oh, no, she's an asylum seeker who comes regularly. Every month we have food from a different country, made by our visitors. We give them the money out of our donations from charitable agencies. Everyone here is either a volunteer, a refugee or both. Some of the volunteers are ex -refugees. The clothes are given to us and sometimes we get toys for the children. We haven't got much money, so we make every penny count."

The whole experience was very comforting and Mary realised that she hadn't thought about her troubles or her mother since she entered the building. This would be a day to look forward to each week.

That evening as they ate their evening meal, Mary asked Mitra about the youth centre she went to. She was curious to see if it compared to the group she'd attended with Giselle.

"Mm, it's alright," was the brief reply.

"But what do you do there?" Mary persisted. "How do you pass the time?"

"Games and things, talking," she answered vaguely, stuffing a large piece of bread in her mouth which prevented any more conversation.

Mary gave up and there was silence for a few minutes until Mitra suddenly said, "Come with me if you want. It's on tomorrow night at six." There was no eye contact and Mitra carried on eating as if she hadn't spoken, but Mary understood the awkwardness of teenagers.

"Mm, ok," Mary answered casually, but her spirits lifted. This was a breakthrough. Perhaps she could make friends with Mitra eventually.

The youth club was in a similar building to the refugee group, large, draughty and busy. Most of the children were English but there were a few foreign faces. Mitra was greeted warmly by her friends and ran off towards a pool table to join a game, leaving Mary to fend for herself. This time she was rescued by a middle aged man wearing a dog collar. "Hallo and welcome." He proffered his hand. "Do you speak English?" His smile was friendly and his voice gentle.

Reassured, Mary asked him about the group. He was only too willing to chat enthusiastically about its formation and aims.

"Really, it started because my own children had nothing to do round here when they were young teenagers. Their friends ended up sprawling on my carpets and settees all summer. When they went out at night I got worried about where they were and what they were doing, especially in winter. So I got this group together. It's a shame it's only one night a week, but I don't have the energy for any more than this."

"You did so well. The children seem to be enjoying themselves." Mary turned her gaze to the pool table, from which shrieks of laughter filled the air. "Mitra looks forward to this every week. I don't know her background yet, but I'm guessing there's bad memories in her life and not much to offset them in the future."

"You're a very caring person, I can see." He smiled benevolently at Mary.

"Thank you. I have a daughter of my own, back in Zimbabwe. She is in my thoughts, always, reverend."

"Please call me Rob. That's what the young people call me. Er – amongst other things I'm not supposed to know about."

"I'm Mary. I'd like to come again, if Mitra allows it. I don't want to embarrass her, but I'm happy to help out here if I could be useful."

"You'll be more than welcome. To me, of course! I can't speak for Mitra."

But, as it turned out, Mitra was pleased with Mary's attention, and even said a gruff "Thanks for coming" as they walked home together. The next day, Mary found the confidence to cook the evening meal. She chose vegetables with herbs and a sprinkling of minced lamb. It was a small step, but she felt a little less like a stranger when the others praised her food.

The following week, Mitra asked casually if Mary was ready to go to the youth club, as they cleared the dishes from the evening meal. Surprised and pleased, Mary hurriedly put on clean clothes and went off to the centre with her.

Soon, it became a weekly routine. They would leave the house after dinner and walk round together. Then Mary would organise and supervise games while Mitra stayed with her friends. Mary found herself listening to problems, sorting out disputes and reassuring the teenagers with anxieties. It was something that benefitted all parties. Meanwhile, the adult group was also becoming a regular outing. Mary had been asked by Flora, the teacher who ran the English classes, if she'd be willing to take a few classes, but the pupils were all young men from an assortment of countries. She said she'd think about it, but secretly found the idea a bit daunting. They all seemed quiet, polite and friendly, but her past experiences made her irrationally cautious.

One evening, when it was her turn to cook the evening meal, Mary broached the subject with Giselle as they chopped vegetables together.

"I've been asked to teach English to some young men at the group. There's ten of them."

"Why not? You'd be perfect. You wanted to do something. C'est une bonne idée. There's nothing to stop you."

Mary hesitated. Could she trust Giselle enough to reveal horrifying incidents in her life? Mitra was in the room, watching television. Although she appeared to be engrossed in the programme, she might overhear.

"I was raped," she said softly, "by a group of young soldiers. It was a revenge thing to hurt my mother."

"That happened to me!" Both women turned round to see that Mitra was staring at them. "It was terrible. I still dream about it sometimes. But I don't mind helping with the teaching. I speak Dari, Farsi and Arabic so I can translate for some of them."

Mary was shocked at Mitra's matter-of-fact tone, but she managed not to show it.

"Can you both come along next week? "

"Mm, suppose so, I've got nothing else to do," Mitra replied nonchalantly.

"I'll be there anyway, so of course I'll help." Giselle was calm and reassuring despite the revelations of her housemates, but didn't prompt any further discussion.

Mary felt a little more positive and useful once the teaching group was in place. The weeks had some routine. Days went by and there were things to do and look forward to. Only the nights were long. The three of them got to know their pupils and share their stories. Then, one week, they arrived at the venue and found the door locked. There was a notice stating that the church had been vandalised so badly that it would be closed for the foreseeable future until funds could be raised for its renovation. Giselle had no idea what it said and Mitra didn't know what vandalised or renovated meant. Only Mary realised the full impact on their little group.

People began turning up and rattling the doors, trying to work out what was going on. Between them, Mary, Mitra and Giselle tried to explain as best they could.

"Come to our house!" Mary offered. "We can do the English lesson, if nothing else."

Four people, glad of something to do, followed them home. That was the first session of the trio's own tutor group.

Chapter Four

It was a normal school day. Sara wandered home through the farm to her Auntie Toto's house. She always walked that way, ever since she was taken there to live just before her mother escaped to England. Auntie Toto was kind, but the house was small and simple compared to the home she was used to. But at least she was safe there and soon her mother would send for her and she could start a new, exciting life. It had been raining, but the sun was out and clouds of steam rose gently from the ground. Her thoughts turned to food and she wondered idly what was for supper.

She didn't notice the three boys, all about her own age, fourteen to fifteen. One of them shouted to her and she realised they had been walking behind her for some time.

"Hey you! I know you. You're from Harare. I've seen your picture! You're that traitor's granddaughter. What are you doing round here?"

She had no idea how they could have seen her photograph, so, after a quick backward glance, she walked on, shaking her head in denial. Surely if she said nothing, they would think they were mistaken.

But one boy persisted, hurling abuse as he got nearer. Sara quickened her steps, her stomach churning. Suddenly the pleasant weather, her hunger, her mother all were forgotten. She sensed the danger these boys were displaying.

"Running away? Too late for that. Come on, you two." The first boy urged his companions on to catch up with Sara and surround her.

"Going home to Amia, are you? She's moved round here, has she? She thought she could hide."

Her heart pounding, she started to run. She was tall and athletic, so streaked away from them. A few moments later, they were out of sight. She heaved a sigh of relief. Her chest was hurting. She slowed down to take a breath.

Then suddenly, the first boy appeared from nowhere, standing in front of her. He grabbed her round the waist, pushing her backwards until she fell to the ground. She heard a scream and realised it had come from her own mouth as he ripped at her clothes, tearing her school shirt and spilling the contents of her satchel. He put a grubby hand over her mouth to stop her shrieking. She tried to bite it. She could feel his hot breath on her face. His body was damp and greasy with sweat. She fought with all her strength, but to no avail. There was a searing pain as he entered her, burning more and more with each thrust.

Then he got up and a second boy took over, while the first one held her arms and shoulders. Fear gave her the strength to try to wriggle away, but it was no use. She couldn't escape. She braced herself for what she knew was coming, and turned her head away to avoid the smell of his breath.

"Come on! Your turn." The third boy was summoned. Sara could see he was hesitating as he stood over her. "Go on!" the other two pushed him on top of her. The weight on her chest crushed her lungs. She wanted to cough but nothing happened. Her head banged against a stone, making her feel dizzy. She closed her eyes. As she did so, the boy whispered in her ear. "Don't open your eyes! Stay still! "

He called across to his friends. "She's not conscious. Leave her. Someone's coming!" The weight lifted from her and she could breathe again. Cool, welcome air filled her lungs, soothing the pain.

She heard their footsteps grow fainter. After a few minutes, she dared to open her eyes. The sun was still shining, the grass was still wet. How, and why had this happened to her? Slowly, she got up. Every inch of her body hurt. She was shivering, though sweat was pouring out of her. But she could still walk. The third boy had probably saved her life.

A nearby field was full of tall crops of maize, high enough to hide a person. Gathering her schoolbooks, she set off through the plants, hidden from the footpath. The straight rows of corn guided her unsteady footsteps. It seemed a long, lonely journey but it felt much safer. Spent of energy, somehow she staggered home.

Auntie Toto saw her coming. “Oh, my god! Oh my god!” was all she could say. But the horror in the expression on her face told Sara how dreadful she looked. A tin bath was filled and Sara gratefully stripped off her uniform and lay in the water, easing her bruises. Exhausted and desolate, she climbed into bed.

Auntie gave her a cup of foul-smelling liquid. “Here, drink this.” It was dark green and full of bits of leaves. It tasted as horrible as it looked. Bravely, Sara drank it without question. Eventually she fell asleep, only to be wakened several hours later with violent stomach cramps. She ran out to the toilet and sat there for what seemed like half the night. When she returned to bed, Auntie had placed a mug of water in reach. It was cold and soothing. By morning she was bleeding heavily. She felt so weak she could hardly move.

“Amia,” she murmured to herself, “please send for me. I need you. I don’t want to die out here.”

Chapter Five

"Say six!" The poor man did his best.

"Sickers"

"No, not sickers! Six!"

"Sick," the man said hesitantly.

"Leave him alone, Mitra. He's trying his best." Mary felt sympathy for the Iraqi speaker desperately attempting the unfamiliar sounds. "Go help Danila. She could do with someone to listen to her reading."

Mitra flounced off with as much bad grace as usual, and Mary took over. "Please don't worry about it, Amir. People will understand your accent. Mitra's very young and impatient."

"It's fine. In my country I helped girls to get to school instead of marrying older men. I'm used to teenage girls. But I was tortured for it. Some people hated me and I had to leave. But I still believe I was right. I am glad Mitra has a voice. She is from Iran. At home, we were enemies once. Here, she is my neighbour."

"We can all be grateful to a man who stood up for us women." Mary was genuinely impressed. Here was a hero indeed. She spent the rest of the session teaching him to interpret slang words she had come across since her arrival in England. He was a quick learner.

There were four students that afternoon. Since the church had closed its doors some weeks ago, the classes at the house had become a highlight for Mary. Her fear of young men lessened as she encountered more and more subdued and injured souls from other countries. Most were ordinary people who were trying to cope with extraordinary circumstances. Helping them made her feel valued. Mitra was supportive, despite her teenage tantrums, and Giselle could speak two African languages as well as excellent French, although her English wasn't good. But she was learning and improving alongside her pupils. Everyone was benefitting from the experience except Hafida, who hid in her room until the visitors had gone.

The four students present that day were eager to get on. Danila was a lady from Pakistan. She had two teenage children who picked up the language from school in a couple of months and did her translating for her. She wanted to start some sort of training so that she could start work as soon as she was allowed to. Collette came from the Cameroons, leaving behind her own and her sister's children when she fled. She spoke fluent French so she was usually Giselle's student. The fourth person was a boy from Afghanistan. He'd met Mitra in the post office while queueing for his allowance. Their native languages were similar, so Mitra was in charge of his progress. His name was Gohar. The little group spent a useful and pleasant couple of hours.

After the guests went home, Mary had an idea as she was preparing the evening meal. At the church, a different country's dish was served every month. Why not introduce this after the lesson, but every week? It was certainly much cheaper to share the cost of ingredients and they could all learn something about each other's culture.

Giselle liked the idea, but Mitra, of course, was sceptical. "I bet the others won't do it. They'll come here and eat the food, then make some excuse when it's their turn."

"They might, but it's worth a try." Mary tried her most persuasive tone. "You may find yourself enjoying it. My Sara loved to cook a meal for me every now and then." Thinking about her daughter brought a deep longing. At least she knew she was safe. Many of her friends here didn't have that reassurance. Covering her sadness, she turned to Giselle for support.

"You're willing to do it, aren't you, Giselle? "

"Bien sur, I would love to do it. I have another idea. Why not ask at the church for money towards the food? They had funds to feed us so there could be some spare now we're not going. It would mean that some people got a free meal."

Even Mitra didn't argue with that proposal. The English studies became cookery, culture and budgeting lessons and a weekly hot meal for the destitute.

Occasionally, a new face would appear at the door, brought by a member of the group, or informed of the project by a friend of a friend. No one was turned away without a hot meal and a sympathetic ear. The church offered a lump sum from their funds, a portion of which was doled out every week to the next cook. There wasn't a bank account so it had to be cash, locked away in a little box given to them by the church treasurer. Mary took charge of the finances. Despite, or maybe, because of its simplicity, the system went well. All the students took a turn and cooked delicious meals which were respectful of all religions. Thursday afternoons became the highlight of the week.

Chapter Six

Amir was pleased to have something to do. He rarely cooked at home. His brother was a chef who owned a restaurant and he usually ate with him in the evenings. It had been a way to keep in touch, until his activities and beliefs became well known. After Amir was given a warning that he would be arrested, his brother, fearing he may be next, sold his business and moved away with his wife and children. They had not seen each other since. Amir was happy they were safe, but he missed them terribly.

The money for the meal didn't stretch very far, and his brother's advice would have been handy as he stood in the world food supermarket, trying to make economic choices. Staple food which was cheap and plentiful at home seemed almost out of reach here. But there were advantages in having a chef in the family. Some of his brother's skills came back to him as he stood in the shop, staring at the goods. Things that he didn't know he knew popped into his mind and soon his imagination had the meal prepared and served within his budget.

This was the first time since he came to England that he'd payed attention to food at all. The group at the church provided the only cooked meal of the month. When that ended, oven chips, crisps and bananas had to do. Hunger forced him out of his flat to the post office and the local supermarket on Wednesdays, but the rest of the week was spent staring at the walls of his flat. But today he realised he felt better for having a purpose, an event to plan.

He spent all morning chopping, peeling, cooking and arranging. He walked the mile trip to Mary's, carrying the food in the plastic cartons given to him for the purpose.

"My, that smells good!" He was greeted at the door by Mary. He felt a flush of pleasure and gratitude. He was used to being praised for his brilliant novels portraying everyday life in Iraq. Here, cooking a meal for others was a simple task, but still fulfilling.

"Perhaps we could do some conversation today, instead of grammar. Talk to me about any subject. I won't interrupt with corrections," Mary said with a smile.

She seemed a caring person. Her voice was soft and her large, clear eyes looked sincere. He believed he could trust her.

"I am from Iraq," he began, hesitantly. "I have been here sickers months, and I still can't say that word!"

They both laughed. Encouraged, Amir stumbled on. "I am a writer. People read my work. They like it. But I wrote about a young girl who wanted to be a doctor. She went to a war zone and her father tried to stop her from helping men who were hurt. She saw men's bodies. She helped lots of people and she trained as a doctor. But she had sex with a man that wasn't known to the family. Her father was ashamed, and people mocked him. It was only a story."

"I think women would love that story of a girl fulfilling her dreams."

"They did. Everyone read it. I was er – how you say?"

"I think you mean famous."

"Famous?"

"It means you were well known."

Spurred on by her interest and understanding, he went on talking. "When I first came to Britain I stayed in my room all the time. I thought someone might recognise me."

"Why did you think that?"

"I was on television, telling women they could have a place in the world, and in other countries, even in our country, things were changing."

"You were a bad influence?"

"What?" he couldn't attempt to say the word back.

"It means you changed people's minds in a bad way."

"I did it for my wife. She was stopped from doing things by her father. She was clever and she was free to do whatever she wanted when she married me, but she died of cancer. I still believe I was right. I would do the same again."

"I am so sorry for your loss. However, I believe you were right. I taught women to read and write, but also to think for themselves and not to accept what they are told if they don't think it is for them. Too many of my friends were married to men who were strangers, but were known to their families who thought they were suitable husbands. Clever girls who earned money had their wages taken by their husbands or fathers. Rich women had a voice. But not us ordinary people. We formed a society. There were thousands of us. It was not just women. Some men joined us, and believed in us. One of them was my husband, who disappeared and we believe he was killed because of his views. My mother was the leader and we marched through Harare. We had women politicians, privileged people who had some influence. Amia tried to get them on side. I helped her. But the government hated her.

"You were a very brave woman. Do I say woman or lady?"

Mary laughed which eased the conversation a little. "Either is fine, in this case. But, just as we thought we were getting somewhere, and our demands were being listened to, my mother was shot dead. I was there at the time. She was standing on a wooden box, surrounded by her followers, urging them to help her lobby the government for a fairer, more equal society. There were hundreds listening and cheering. Suddenly, she fell to the ground."

There was a horrified silence. Amir watched Mary's face crumple as she dealt with her terrible memories.

"I'm so sorry," he managed to say. He hated to upset this lovely person.

"It's ok. Everybody here has lost family members. Hafida still sobs all night and can't talk to anyone. I lost my husband fifteen years ago. He was a hero, too. We were never quite sure what happened to him, but he ran away to protect me and my baby. I still miss him but at least I'm fairly normal. Thoughts of my daughter keep me going. She's living in a village with a relative where no one knows us. I made her aunt, my husband's sister, memorise my address. I sent it as soon as I moved in."

"I was very depressed," Amir confessed. "I arrived here and lay in bed all day. I was given pills but I hid them from myself in case I took them all one bad day."

"I know that feeling. But I have a daughter who is waiting for me to send for her. I can't let her down."

"How is she? Do you hear from her?"

"I told them not to contact me unless something goes wrong. Mail and phones get stolen. But I'm sure you understand. It must happen in your country."

This woman actually understood him! He had been so wrapped up in his own problems, but it was a good feeling to have concerns for someone else.

The session came to an end, and the food was a great success. Giselle offered to cook next time. All the class said goodbye and went their different ways. Amir reached his little home, but somehow, it didn't seem so lonely after all.

Chapter Seven

Back at his flat, Amir felt happier and more interested in life than he had done since he first came to England. The dishes he'd used to make the meal were scattered around the kitchen. Immediately he set about cleaning up. Usually he ignored housework when he came home, or didn't even notice that things needed doing until several days had passed. Now he started the tasks with energy, humming as he worked and going over his conversation with Mary in his mind. It was the first time he'd shared such intimate things and found he was able to express himself in another language.

He was in his home for an hour before he remembered to put on the radio. On other days, he flicked the switch as soon as he walked in. Even if he couldn't find a station he could understand, the sound of another voice in the room was comforting. It was a cheap set that someone gave him as an afterthought, instead of throwing it away, but to him it became a treasured possession.

Perhaps he could volunteer to cook every Thursday. Everyone was so pleased with his efforts and it was wonderful to be praised, albeit for such a small thing. At home, he had hundreds, if not thousands of followers, despite his notoriety with the government. Now his fan base was smaller and less complex, but he found he appreciated it just as much.

Mary was washing up in her home at the same time as Amir. Giselle helped her and Mitra sprawled in front of the television. Hafida ate a portion of food in her room.

"Mitra, can you get Hafida's dishes?" Mary called. "We've nearly finished."

"I took the plates up. It's somebody else's turn. Anyway, she can come down."

"Please? You're not doing anything."

With a dissatisfied sigh, Mitra went to the foot of the stairs and yelled "Hafida" followed by a torrent of Farsi.

"Don't speak to her like that!" remonstrated Mary.

"You don't know what I said." Mitra retorted. "I just told her they'd all gone, that's all."

She slumped back on the settee, arms folded in a defiant gesture. But a few minutes later, Hafida appeared in the doorway, handed the dishes over and scurried back upstairs. Mary felt that she had at least achieved something. Suddenly she realised how much she'd enjoyed Amir's company. A short encounter had pushed her pain and anxiety to the corner of her mind. Once the chores were finished, her troubles crept back into the forefront. To ease the pain, she thought about Amir. She hadn't noticed before, but he was quite attractive. He was around her age, early forties, tall and willowy, with a kind, strong face. There was a sadness in his eyes. It was an expression she saw often in the faces of her companions.

As she closed her eyes that night, her mother's face appeared, smiling down at her. Mary was a child again, for a brief moment, feeling safe and protected. She woke the next morning. Everything was the same as before. Hafida was crying softly, and through the window she saw the man with the ponytail making his way to work in the rain. Just another day. But somehow, this strange life began to make some sense.

It was a whole week before they were to meet up again, and for Amir, it seemed too long a time. Days passed slowly in this peculiar life of waiting for something to happen, with nothing but memories to think about. Friday was Amir's day to report to the immigration centre so at least that meant he had to leave the house and use his bus pass to get across town. The pass could only be used for that one journey, but at least it was somewhere to go. On the way back, a man greeted him in Kurdish and fell into step as he approached the bus stop.

Hey, how are you? I spoke to you last time we came here. Do you remember?"

Amir didn't, but pretended to, desperately trying to recall the man's face. He felt more confident now after the successful encounter at Mary's, so he allowed the man to chat away until, somewhere at the back of his mind, he realised when he'd seen him before. It was at his last visit to the immigration centre.

"If you're interested, I can get you a bit of money, at the warehouse, in town. All illegal, of course, but there's not much risk of being found out. They take you on at weekends, when the place is closed, so we're safe from snoopers. The money's not much, but if you're sending it home, it's useful."

"I haven't anyone left at home," Amir replied, reluctantly. "My wife died soon after we were married and we had no children."

"Well, a few extras, then. The boss speaks Kurdish and he's been here for years. He knows the system."

It was fraught with risks, but Amir felt tempted. If he was found out, it might mean the end of his bid for asylum. Everything he'd endured up until now would be wasted and he'd be back home, probably locked up, or worse. But he was lonely and knew the companionship would make him feel better. If he didn't tell anyone, who would know? Perhaps it was worth a shot. And, after all, he wasn't doing anything else. The man could see that Amir was hesitating. "I'm Abdul. If you want it, come down Sunday morning, to the Square, and join us. We'll be sitting on the steps at 7 o'clock. Might see you there."

He was young, and his face was innocent and enthusiastic. Could he be trusted? People caught working were put in prison, he knew. He was trying hard to keep out of trouble to make his case more favourable. But time stretched before him until Thursday when he was due at Mary's again.

The following Sunday found him sitting in the Square alongside several men, all sleepy and dressed in shabby work clothes. Abdul greeted him warmly. "You should have put your old things on. You might spoil those trousers."

"I haven't anything else. I came here with one set of everything to change into."

"You need to go to charity shops, or better still, find places where clothes are given away. It doesn't matter what they look like here." He pulled a pair of baggy nylon tracksuit bottoms from his rucksack. "Put these on over your own."

Amir did as he was told, grateful for the concern shown. He saw Abdul glance at his hands and realised his friend knew he wasn't used to manual work. However, nothing was exchanged but a reassuring smile. Amir's doubts about trusting this person were slowly being dispelled.

Soon, a large, rusty van rattled past and parked round the corner. In twos and threes the men drifted off in different directions but all ended up at the van, where they were herded in and taken to the warehouse. In the corner of a huge high-ceilinged storeroom were piles of stout cardboard crates divided into sections inside. The windows were covered in dust and moss, which gave them protection from prying eyes, but made the vast room dark and eerie inside. Occasionally a rat scuttled across the floor and disappeared into a hole in the corner. Apart from that, they were undisturbed.

Their task was to stick labels on some oddly shaped bottles full of a brown, clear liquid. One of the bottles leaked a dribble of something with a strange odour. The boss hurriedly came over when he was aware of the smell and screwed the top more securely. The labels said "whisky" but the mixture smelled nothing like the whisky he'd encountered in English and American circles at home. Amir knew it was alcohol but he couldn't identify it any further. He wondered if the others, many of whom couldn't understand the language, had any idea what they were doing.

They worked all day. Amir didn't have food with him, so when they stopped work for a short break, he sat alone, watching the others eat.

"Here, share mine." His new acquaintance came to sit beside him and offered him a spiced boiled egg, some okra and a pitta bread with a hummus dip. It was the first time since Amir had cooked for Mary that he'd tasted such delicious food. The okra and dip made him unbearably homesick. He felt like a child again, watching his mother pound chickpeas, oil and herbs in their kitchen at home.

The sharp taste of the okra set off the smooth blend of the hummus and Amir could identify the coriander and lemon juice which made up some of the ingredients.

His companion watched him with interest. "Have a drink." He offered him the cup from a flask. It contained hot, sweet tea that almost burned his throat on the way down.

"You're Amir, aren't you? You'll feel better for that." Abdul smiled benignly as he drank the rest of the tea direct from the flask.

At dusk, they were told to gather up the boxes of whisky and stack them into the van. They were not allowed any artificial light for this, which made it all the more difficult. The boss handed out a twenty-pound note to each man, then drove off, leaving them to find their own way back. It was now nine o'clock at night.

"Come on, I'll show you the way." Abdul walked beside him until they reached the Square again. "Will you come again? It won't be as bad next time. You'll know what to expect."

Despite his initial reservations, Amir warmed to this man and felt grateful for his friendship and that of the other workers. Not everyone spoke Amir's language, but there was a camaraderie which he'd never enjoyed since coming to England, except at Mary's. Back at his flat that night, his back was aching and his hands were sore, but his brain was relaxed and calm for the first time.

Chapter Eight

The Thursday group prospered and many people came and went and found friendship, hot food and English lessons. Mary felt that there was something to carry on for, though it wasn't at all what she'd imagined she'd be doing when she moved to England.

Summer turned up unexpectedly in this unpredictable climate. After months of rain and cold winds, she awoke one day to sunshine and warmth. The rooftops viewed through her bedroom window sparkled and the man with the ponytail whistled on his way to work. Instead of shades of grey, there were pinks, yellows and greens sticking up from the cracks in the cobbles as tiny flowers bravely raised their heads.

Summer wasn't the only surprise of the day. Just as Mary and Giselle were clearing away the breakfast dishes, Flora, the group manager from the church came round. "I've got some news."

Mary and Giselle looked anxiously at each other. "Oh, no, have we run out of money? The Thursdays are going so well. Our friends will really miss them. We're always getting new people who don't know anyone here, and we help them cope." Mary's heart sank as she said the words. "In fact, we were hoping that one day we could go back to meeting at the church, and be able to get more people involved. Will we have to close this as well?"

"No, it's not that, though it's not good news there either. I may have to try for more funding soon. But this is better news. A socicty who usually pays for an outing every year for our visitors, has given us some money. I've got the cash, but no group. Would you two be able to organise it? I'll help, of course. They need feedback for their members so it will have to be spent on a trip and it must also be evaluated."

"That's a great idea!" Mary was relieved and filled with enthusiasm.

"Where can we go?" asked Giselle.

"I suggest a nice park in a small market town that's only half an hour's train journey away. The park's in the centre and it has a swimming pool, a children's railway and a playground. If you can spread the word amongst your clients, I still have a few phone numbers. But lots of people will have moved on since I closed my group."

"I see my Congolese friends every week at church. We are a strong community. And Mitra goes to the youth club. She's still in bed at the moment but I'll tell her," Giselle said.

"I still go to the youth club with Mitra, and we may get help from the vicar. He's keen on giving the kids other views of the country," Mary said.

"Let me know numbers, at least as accurately as you can. In the past, we always got more than we bargained for."

"We'll use our food money to buy picnic food to take with us and ask everyone to bring something." Mary was excited to have a new project to plan.

"Well, I don't think there will be much more food money to come." The manager replied. "Sadly, the church wants all funds to go on repairs from now on as we're having great difficulty with payments. But as I said, I'm going to try for more for your project."

This was bad news along with the good. Mary put it to the back of her mind, hoping there might be something they could do to keep going. Meanwhile, she had an outing to organise.

A week later, fifty children and adults and several kilos of food piled into railway carriages and were on the way to their escape. Amir was given the task of organising the food. Everyone cooked something and vegetable curry, chicken biryani, tilapia fish, tomato rice and stuffed vine leaves augmented the conventional English picnic fare of sandwiches and cakes. Blankets were wrapped round hot cooking pots and baby buggies were used to ferry their belongings.

Seeing other families with their children pierced Mary's heart with a surge of loneliness. She missed her daughter so much. She consoled herself by thinking about the joyful time when she could send for her. At least she was safe in the country with her aunt.

They were blessed with a beautiful day. Bright sunshine lit up the flowers, trees and grass. It was a rare reprieve from the normal greyness of the English climate. Immediately they arrived, children were grabbing balls and playing football on the sweeping lawns and racing each other to the swings and roundabouts. Mitra's teenage friends joined in with the little ones and were soon shrieking like five-year-olds. The adults sat around on the grass, relaxing and chatting. Amir saw Mary watching the children and came over to sit beside her.

"Thank you, Mary for all your care, and the others as well." He wasn't sure he was using the correct words so he took her hand and squeezed it gently.

"Oh, please, no need to thank me! I've enjoyed all this. I'd have nothing to do if I didn't do this. I don't know how we're going to carry on providing food without the money but we'll have to try. People rely on it now." She didn't release his hand. Amir was tempted to tell her about his job, but at the last minute decided not to. He couldn't bear for her to think badly of him. They sat in companionable silence for a few moments, observing the others enjoying their day.

Then Amir tentatively asked, "Would you like to visit me at my house? I could cook for you. It would be good to have someone inside."

It was a quaint way to ask for a date, but Mary appreciated the effort to find the words. "Yes, I'd like that," she smiled. "When would you want me to come?"

"On Monday?" Amir knew he'd have his money from work.

"Alright, Monday it is." She tried not to sound too eager. Inside, she was in a chaos of conflicting emotions. She wanted so much to be close to someone but had an overwhelming fear of physical contact after the brutal treatment she'd endured in Zimbabwe.

At dusk, the party ended and they all drifted back to the railway station, tired, happy and gossiping together.

Mary busied herself by making sure everyone had their tickets, the children or parents or friends they came with. There were no dramas and everyone travelled home together. She noticed Mitra was on the arm of a tall, dark-haired boy of around sixteen years old. He had an East European accent.

He had a slight stoop and a hesitant demeanour. Her concern for Mitra was something to concentrate on. She could hear the conversation and saw Mitra's flirting, confident manner. But the unease about the visit to Amir's kept rising above all other thoughts and just wouldn't go away.

Amir set off at seven o'clock on Sunday morning and hung around the square as usual. His friend Abdul appeared at his side, bright and cheerful.

"Great news!" he told Amir in Kurdish. "I now have enough money to send for my wife and children. They might be here in a few weeks! I can pay someone at home to get them out of the country."

"That's wonderful news." Amir was genuinely thrilled for his friend, recognising how lonely he must be. Abdul must live very frugally to have saved up from the meagre allowance and wages he received. He was also envious that this person had a family to worry about. The van arrived and a couple of the men sitting around got up. Abdul followed.

"See you in there." He whispered as he passed. Amir waited the necessary five minutes and then got up to join them. As he did so he heard Abdul's voice shouting "No! Leave me alone!" Amir realised it was a warning. He looked round the corner and saw Abdul struggling to escape from the grasp of three policemen. A fourth was racing down the street after their boss, who was streaking away almost out of sight. Quickly he returned to the square, which was now empty of his comrades. He ran as fast as he could in the opposite direction of the arrest. Once away from the square he had the sense to slow down and walk normally, trying not to attract attention.

He took the long way home, half expecting the police to be waiting at his doorstep. He was annoyed with himself for taking the risk in the first place. It may jeopardise his case. There was no way he could go back home to Iraq, and now he might not get leave to remain here, if there was an excuse to throw him out. He wanted the money to buy food to cook a nice meal for Mary. Apart from a few vegetables, there was nothing in the fridge.

But that proved to be the least of his worries. A couple of hours later he received a text from Abdul. He'd been told it was likely that he would be put in jail for his part in illegal manufacture of alcohol and fraud. Amir felt grateful and guilty at the same time at having escaped when Abdul was locked up. His friend's warning cries saved him. Just as his life was improving, Abdul's plans had been set back and may have been completely destroyed.

The next day found him confessing all to Mary as he prepared a meagre dinner of rice, carrots and onions. After they'd eaten, she tried to comfort him.

"It's not your fault. It's just bad luck that he went first. He called out to save you and the others. You'd have done the same."

"But he needed the money," Amir answered. "I only wanted the company and some food to make a nice meal."

He was relieved and pleased that she wasn't in any way judgemental. He wanted to tell her this, but couldn't find the words. Eventually he said, "You are a very good person. A good person to me."

"I'm not used to men being kind to me." Mary confessed. "My husband was my only man and he died when my daughter was a baby. He was strong and brave, like my mother. Since then I 've never been with anyone else."

"I lost my wife to cancer. I thought I would be alone forever. But you are a lovely person. You can make me happy just by smiling at me."

She held out her arms for an embrace and he held her close. He noticed she was shaking.

"Don't be afraid of me," he whispered. She didn't reply, but, still trembling, pulled him closer.

Chapter Nine

Mary stayed the night at Amir's. She fell asleep feeling happy, relaxed and wanted. However, she woke the next day with no idea where she was. She could feel the warmth and smell the presence of another person, but for a second, she couldn't remember how she got there. Through the eleven storey window there was nothing but sky and clouds. Muffled sounds of movements somewhere below sounded eerily sinister. A sense of terror overtook her and suddenly, she sat bolt upright, gazing around the room.

"It's alright, don't be afraid." Her rapid movements had awakened Amir, who was staring at her. "I'm not that bad, am I? I know I'm not very pretty, but..."

"Sorry, I didn't realise where I was. I've had so many changes. The silliest things scare me." His smile reassured her and the memories of a lovely day came flooding back. "I slept so well. At home, the nights are full of bad dreams. I had such a nice time with you."

"I tried to make it up to you with love after such a small meal. You must be really hungry."

"I'm ravenous!"

"What does that mean?"

"It means so hungry you could eat anything, whether it was edible or not."

"Edible?"

"Never mind."

"What?"

At that she gave up trying to explain and instead, pulled him towards her and hugged him tight. The English lesson could wait awhile.

"I have tea. I will make you one."

He went onto the kitchen and was moving about in there for several minutes. She had almost forgotten about the task when he reappeared carrying a plate with two cups and a milk carton balanced precariously on it.

“Oh, how nice” she started to say when suddenly, Amir tripped and fell onto the bed, spilling the contents of the tray all over the duvet. His crestfallen face was so funny that Mary couldn’t help laughing out loud, and, after a moment, Amir joined in and they rolled around happily together amongst the wet bedclothes. Mary felt she had never laughed so much since her carefree childhood. She savoured the feeling and tucked it away in her mind to bring out later in less pleasant times.

“I’ll have to go soon,” Mary said apologetically “I’m sorry to leave you with all this clearing up to do but I must get back. I promised Mitra that I’d show her how to cook and I also want to do a few chores. In return for the cooking lessons I said I would go to the youth centre with her on Friday. I’d go with her anyway, but it gives her an incentive.”

“How did that start?” asked Amir.

“Well, I asked her, and, though she tried not to show it, I could tell she wanted me to come. I needed something to do and I like young people. I’ve always worked with them. Mitra has been a member for a long time and I’m trying to get close to her. I miss my daughter and she’s the same age. They’re not alike, though.”

“You are a kind lady.”

“It’s a selfish reason, really. And sometimes I’m not so kind, sometimes I hate my mother. She was so passionate about injustice that she died for it. I’m only alive because I sold everything I had to come here, where I can’t work, I’m always cold, and I have no family...“

“You have me now, Mary, for as long as you want me.”

He sounded so sincere that Mary felt a little ashamed of the way she’d spoken.

“At least I know what happened to my mother. Lots of her followers disappeared. Anyway I’ll go home and get on with a few tasks and give Mitra her lessons.”

“Can I come on Friday as well? I could help with the children. My days are empty now,” Amir said tentatively.

“Why not? I could use another pair of hands. So could Rob, the vicar. He’s very welcoming.”

“Even to a Muslim?”

Mary smiled. "All faiths respected, but they're mostly Christian, though there are some youngsters from other countries and cultures. You'll fit right in. For today I have a plan. I'll help you clear up here, then you come round to mine and we'll do the chores together. Perhaps you could teach Mitra how to make some of the Kurdish food you've given us"

"That would be good." Amir felt useful for once. He would have something to do and he would be able to spend time with Mary. He wasn't sure how he'd get on with teenagers, but he was more than willing to give it a try. Any human contact was welcome.

He seemed so pleased to be invited to do small tasks. His almost hesitant manner, no doubt acquired by his treatment in his own country, was somehow appealing to Mary. She was used to her mother's pioneering spirit and undaunted enthusiasm for justice for her people. Nothing cooled Amia's passion, and her many followers said she must have born with her fist in the air. She died as she lived, protesting against cruel treatment and inequalities around her. Not everyone was so brave. But there were other ways to show courage. She respected Amir's quiet, resolute passion for his cause.

The following Friday saw the three of them setting off together to the youth club. Mary could tell that Amir was a little bit apprehensive, but said nothing.

Mitra was as nonchalant as ever when she learned that Amir was to accompany them to the youth club. But there was no objections to the plan, which Mary took as a good sign. The trio were greeted warmly by the vicar, Rob.

"I'm always on the lookout for volunteers. People come and go, but there are a few of us that have been here since I started the project. New faces tend to have new ideas and bring a freshness to the group."

"I will try my best," replied Amir. "The only young people I was involved with at home were my brother's children. They drew me into all their activities."

"You have children of your own?" vicar enquired.

“Sadly, no. My wife died very soon after we married. She inspired me to think about women’s rights. I wrote novels and films about it.”

“Well I hope you like us! You’re very welcome. But I have to take some details from you to make sure there is no reason to prevent you from mixing with people under the age of eighteen. It’s a safety rule in this country. Mary already went through the same process.”

Amir readily agreed and passed a happy two hours joining in with games, refereeing football in the church gardens and serving refreshments. The three of them walked home together, tired but content in each other’s company. Mary noticed that Amir’s nervousness had disappeared.

They were almost home when a car passed, revving its engine as loudly as possible. A youth poked his head out of the window and screamed “Dirty nigger, Fuck off!” The car then roared away into the distance, leaving Mary and Amir shocked and frightened. A few seconds later it returned on the other side of the road, this time with the driver yelling “I hate you lot...” The rest of the speech went unheard as they sped off. Mary clung to Amir in fear, and noticed he tried to shield her and Mitra, pushing them behind him in case of attack. Only Mitra remained unperturbed.

“They won’t do anything,” she reassured the others. “It’s all talk. They’ve done it to me loads of times, shouting ‘asylum seeker’ at me but then they run away.” She shrugged a disinterested shoulder. “They’re cowards, really, showing off.”

“In my country, there’s violence if people don’t like you,” said Amir “People don’t mix without disapproval. Prejudice is common.”

“The same in my home,” added Mary. “You’re not allowed to think differently, never mind look different. I just didn’t expect it here.”

“A marriage to someone with a different religion can make you an outcast or even get you killed in my country. That’s one of the things I wrote about,” said Amir.

"Do you think it won't happen here?" snorted Mitra scornfully. "Stay away from your own kind if you two want to stay together. I found out the hard way. Some people's views don't change just because they're in a different country"

They walked on in silence, each busy with their own thoughts. The incident unnerved Mary, but later she remembered that Amir had tried to shield her because he thought she was in danger. He may not be as brave as her mother, but he'd wanted to protect her. She warmed to him more than ever.

And Mitra was right. There was so much prejudice in the world. People who looked different were sometimes avoided just for that reason. Mary realised that Mitra had learned many adult lessons in her young life.

Chapter Ten

The youth club quickly became a routine outing for the three of them, from which they all benefitted. Mary and Amir enjoyed doing something together and spent hours discussing the new friends they made among the teenagers. Mitra merely tolerated their presence at first, but after a while she was comfortable enough to share worries and even to ask advice now and again. All too soon the days got shorter and they were walking to the church through golden yellow leaves strewn across the pavements, pulling their coats around them for protection from wind and rain.

"How long does this go on?" asked Mary as they struggled home in the dark in November, with hailstones blowing towards them and stinging their faces.

"Only just started!" said Mitra cheerfully. "Sometimes it snows but it doesn't last long. That's what they tell me, anyway. I was here last year, and it snowed then. The rain's worse, though. You get wet, then you can't get warm again."

"I wonder how my daughter will cope," Mary said, half to herself.

"She'll have to get used to it, if she's going to stay. That's if she manages to get here in the first place." Mitra, tactless as ever, tossed the remark into the air without looking at Mary.

Amir saw the sadness in Mary's eyes and put a protective arm around her.

"Well, it's getting harder and harder to get into this country." Mitra carried on regardless. "There's all these new rules now. And they can get rid of you very quickly when you do arrive. I've been thinking of a plan to make sure I won't be sent back."

"What plan?" Despite her distress, Mary was curious.

“I’m going to get pregnant. I’ve heard you can’t be sent back if you have a baby. The baby’s a British citizen. You could try it yourself.”

“I can’t have another child, Mitra. Something happened to me when I was assaulted and it can’t be put right. That’s why my Sara is precious.”

“Oh, sorry about that,” Mitra prattled on. ”Just me, then.”

“Who will be the father?” Amir asked.

“Rafal from the youth club. He already wants sex with me. I said no, but I might consider it.”

“Please think about this,” Mary pleaded. “You shouldn’t just rush into these things.”

“Well, I don’t want to go back. I’ve no family left. There’s no house for me to go to. It was sold to pay my fare. Why not do it? How hard can it be?”

Mary was unable to come up with a reply, but Amir said, gently, “Let’s ask Giselle when we get home. She’s been here longer than us and she knows a lot of people. She might be able to help.”

“Mm, suppose so,” was the only response, but it was better than nothing. Both Mary and Amir accepted it and no more was said until they got home.

Back at the house, Giselle listened calmly to Mitra’s plan. “It’s not easy. A baby is a person. It’s not a thing. You can’t go off to youth club to see your friends. It will be by your side all the time. But I have heard your plan many times since I came to this country. Lots of girls have had babies to stay in the country. I have been in a detention centre. It was a mistake, so they let me out again. I must tell you, while I was there, I saw lots of people with babies, waiting to be sent back to their homelands. They weren’t allowed to stay just because they had a child.”

“Oh, no! That can’t be right!”

“I’m afraid it is. But you have a chance of getting leave to remain on your own, if you can be patient. As much chance as two of you would have, anyway.”

Mitra turned away, despondent, and threw herself face down on the settee.

Mary tried to comfort her. "When you're allowed to stay, you can get a job, or go to college, and have a baby later. Things will work out."

"I want to know I'm here to stay. Not forever, but at least to settle somewhere. I don't like waiting."

"None of us do. We all hate waiting. We know how you feel." Amir's tone was gentle and soothing.

Mary joined in the conversation. "I'm waiting to see my Sara again. It's almost unbearable at times. But we can help each other through it."

Despite trying to hide it, the others could see that Mitra enjoyed the support. "I suppose that this must be what it's like to have parents, bossing you about." But she was smiling as she said it.

Chapter Eleven

It was a bad winter. Mary had only seen snow in films and even though she hated the cold, she was looking forward to the beautiful views of white carpets and heavily laden cotton wool trees. Alas, it was not to be. The discomfort of freezing weather had no redeeming feature. Instead of making pretty pictures, strong winds blew rain and hailstones to attack them. Rain turned to ice overnight, melted in the day, then turned to ice again, making roads and pavements treacherous. But the intrepid trio were not put off. Although they shivered, their weekly jaunts to Rob's youth club were too precious to stay in.

The adults' English lessons continued and the midday meal was usually hot soup made of vegetables to keep the pupils warm for the journey home. Most of them had nowhere else to go except the local library so the lessons were a trip out to be enjoyed even in the cold weather. It gave Mary a purpose, something to look forward to each Thursday.

Friday was her favourite day, however. Being among the youngsters reminded her of the school she used to work in, and the daughter she missed so much.

At the church youth club, Christmas was celebrated by all visitors, regardless of religious beliefs. Vicar Rob wisely concentrated on the similarities between faiths, rather than the differences. Members of the club were invited to the midnight service on Christmas Eve, but it was mentioned once only.

"Do you think we ought to go?" asked Mary as they walked home together from the club.

"It's against my religion to attend the service. I've done lots of things my country disapproves of. I don't want Allah against me also," Amir answered.

"I'll go with you," Mitra said cheerfully. "My country doesn't care about me, and this country doesn't either. But here, in this church, they care. They look after me."

Mary put a protective arm around Mitra's shoulders. For once, Mitra didn't shrug her off, but hugged Mary's waist as they walked along.

On Christmas Eve, they went to church in the rain. Neither woman was used to being out so late at night, so they linked arms for comfort. Rob's sermon was all about peace, love and inclusion. It was short, down to earth and in simple but not patronising language. Rob spoke to each person as they left, and was pleased to see Mary and Mitra file out with the rest.

"Many thanks for coming. And for your help at the club." Rob smiled kindly at them.

"We both enjoyed it, didn't we?" Mary turned to Mitra for confirmation, who grunted in reply. "It was a lovely service. I so enjoyed your sermon," Mary went on, regardless of Mitra's indifference.

Rob smiled and moved on to the next worshippers.

"Why didn't you speak to him?" Mary asked.

"Dunno," was the only reply. But she took Mary's arm again as they left the church.

Outside the church gates a familiar figure was waiting. Amir stood, huddled against the wall to protect himself from the cold.

"Oh, that's nice of you to come for us!" Mary said gratefully.

"I wanted to look after my girls," was the response. Together they headed back. "I've got an idea. I've got some food in at my house. Let's have a big meal tomorrow at yours and we can all cook something. There was lots of cheap food at the supermarket this afternoon so I got as much as I could afford." Amir seemed excited at giving them a Christmas dinner. "It won't be like other people's meals. How do you say that, the usual food?"

"I think you mean traditional," answered Mary. "That sounds wonderful whatever we eat. Our customs are all different anyway."

The Christmas dinner was a great success. Giselle and Mary contributed to the preparations, but Amir did the main part. Some of the food was completely new to them, but they tried everything. Sprouts, mince pies, parsnips were served alongside stuffed vine leaves, tomato rice and fried plantains. Sausages wrapped in bacon were also on the menu, but they were a step too far for Amir. Even Hafida sat at the table across from Amir and pecked at some rice and a vine leaf.

Mitra announced that they should all shake hands and Hafida offered a trembling hand to Amir. He took it in both his, and for a long second they stared at one another. Then Hafida shivered visibly and got up and rushed upstairs. Her companions didn't try to detain her.

"At least she joined us for a little while," said Giselle "It's the first time."

"She's terrified of men," Mitra added, nonchalantly.

"How do you know that?" Mary asked.

"She told me months ago not to let men in the house. But I took no notice."

Mary sighed. Though Mitra's apparent disregard sounded heartless, the request was impossible to grant, as the housing officers had a right to inspect the property at any time, and they were all male.

After the meal, Hafida stayed in her room. The others watched television in comfortable silence save for the odd remark or burst of laughter. They all felt homesick, and they all knew the others were feeling it too. Mitra sat by Mary on the sofa and linked her arm. Mary said nothing, but looked across at Giselle, who smiled into Mary's eyes. Mary saw Sara's face, trying to smile on the last occasion she saw her. It was comforting to remember she was safe with Toto, but she longed to have her sitting at her side, on the sofa.

The weeks went on with no word from the home office. They signed on at the detention centre every fortnight, collected money from the post office every week, hosted the English group on Thursdays and helped at the youth club on Fridays. Although the temperature hovered above freezing on most days, the nights were becoming shorter, giving fresh hope to the waiting game. Life seemed that bit more pleasant. But, just as the crocuses and daffodils brightened up the window boxes in the town centre, Giselle heard some bad news. The government had decided that the Congo was now safe for the return of its asylum seekers in Britain. Her friends at her church assured her that relatives at home were disputing this, and warning them to stay away. Apparently, murders and imprisonment were happening regularly. The whole Congolese community was feeling very unsafe.

One evening in March, Giselle asked Mary and Amir to help her with a protest march which her friends at her church were trying to organise. "We're not sure what to do. If we march around without telling anyone, we are told we could be arrested. Who do we go to?"

Amir's experience with the law made him cautious of giving advice. "My friend is in prison now and I would be, too if he hadn't warned me to run away. I'm not the person to ask."

But Mary knew where to get an answer. "The vicar will tell us. I'll ask at the youth club."

This seemed to be a good idea, so the subject was broached at the next session.

"I've no clue how to organise it, but I certainly know where to go," Rob said confidently. "A close friend is a member of an anti-racist group which holds demonstrations all the time. Get him on board and I'm sure he'd love to help."

The information was invaluable. Within a few days of asking, a meeting was held with Martin, the vicar's friend, who involved the rest of his colleagues. Giselle's friends and the congregation from her church got together to discuss procedure with the experts. Routes were mapped out, dates were set and jobs were allocated. There was a buzz of excitement and a sense of purpose and hope. Everyone was looking forward to the event.

They set off on a cold, blustery day in March. Despite the discomfort, there was a feeling of optimism in the air. This was an adventure. The students of the English class at Mary's came along to support the cause, as did several of the young people from the youth club. Amir would have liked to invite the workers he met from the illegal alcohol project, but he guessed they were trying to keep out of sight if possible. He took the risk himself, but couldn't expect anyone else to do it.

The organisers were busy handing out leaflets and getting people to sign petitions on behalf of individuals who had made contributions to society during their stay in the U.K. Fifty pence bought a packet of sandwiches from a young entrepreneur and drinks from flasks of tea and coffee were shared out. The police took up positions in the street, and after much shouting, gossiping and hustle and bustle, they set off. At least one hundred Congolese attended the march, and soon they were singing loudly in Lingala along the way. These were adults and children who had suffered horrors and tragedies in the past, and now faced a very uncertain future. But this was a fun day out, and they made the most of it.

Mary, Amir and Mitra had no idea what the song was about, but soaked up the carefree atmosphere nonetheless. There were buzz words being yelled out in English during breaks from the song.

It was going well for the trio until the marching turned to dancing. Without warning, the crowd began moving from side to side in time with their own singing. Amir was no dancer, and almost fell over several times while trying to keep up. Then, suddenly, everyone reversed their steps and Mary and Mitra were pushed backwards by the huge bottoms of two large ladies in front. The three friends couldn't stop laughing, and despite the seriousness of the reasons for the demonstration, Mary was having great fun.

Amir, used to the more dignified procedure of protest by the written word, found himself shouting slogans loudly whenever appropriate, which occurred often. But Mitra benefitted the most. All her frustrations and anger managed to find an outlet among like-minded people who appreciated her sentiments instead of being irritated by them. Screaming "Congo not safe!" to the world in general was a liberating experience she'd never had before. In the heat of the moment she trod on the foot of tall, lanky teenager who was marching alongside her.

“Hey, watch it!” He had long, floppy, dark brown hair and stooped slightly. He was smiling as he bent down to look at her. “Hi, Mitra! We haven’t spoken much since the picnic last summer. You ok?”

He had a shy but welcoming manner that even Mitra couldn’t object to.

“I didn’t do it on purpose. I didn’t know it was you, or I might have done.” She gave a sidelong flirty glance in his direction. “What are you doing here, anyway?”

“My best friend is from the Congo,” he answered. “I don’t want him to go back and be killed. He’s been here since he was two. He hasn’t got relatives there. They’re all dead. His parents are here with him. He doesn’t remember anything about his country. He’s always round at our house.”

“What do your parents think?”

“They don’t mind. They love him. He makes them laugh. I go to his house sometimes. His mum and dad are fun too. They’re all at the front, leading the way. ”

Mitra was full of curiosity. “Can I meet them?”

“Yes, sure! We’ll go up to them when the march is over.”

They fell into step, yelling and chanting along in harmony.

“What’s your name? I’ve forgotten.”

“It’s Lazlo.”

“Oh yes, I remember it was something silly.”

“It’s not silly in Poland. It’s an ordinary name.” He grinned at her, not in the least offended.

Mitra felt at ease with him. His pleasant manner made him good company. They marched on together until they reached the city square, where the march ended. Lazlo met up with his Congolese friends, and Mitra found them just as entertaining and jolly as Lazlo described them.

“This is Mitra, a friend from the youth club. She’s from Iran.” Lazlo greeted a stocky teenage boy with skin so dark it almost matched his short, black curly hair. His broad smile and sparkling eyes lit up his animated face.

“I’m Paul. Glad you’re supporting us,” he said cheerfully. “Lazlo’s always asking me to come to the group. Perhaps I will, now." He turned to a man and woman carrying a banner between them. They were both laughing and performing an impromptu dance on the spot.

"Here's my mum and dad! This is Mitra from Iran, helping us with the struggle."

The parents put down the banner to shake hands. "I'm Pierre and this is Micheline. Pleased to meet you." His beaming smile was as bright and wide as his son's. Then they picked up the banner again and carried on dancing on the spot.

Mitra couldn't help saying, "You're so cheerful, yet this is so serious."

"Pierre answered, "We will win or die. We have done nothing wrong. See!" he pointed to the banner, which read, 'Claiming asylum is not a crime!' "We will fight with all our strength."

With that they boogied off round the square. People were making speeches, handing out petitions and buying food from homemade trays. But soon, enthused by Micheline and Pierre's antics, most people joined in and danced off up the road. Paul rolled his eyes in his parent's direction, then with a tolerant shrug, waved goodbye and followed them, a cheeky grin on his face.

Mitra and Lazlo sat down on the steps where Amir and Abdul used to wait for their illegal workforce. Eventually, Amir found them and offered to walk Mitra home.

"It's ok I can find my own way back. I don't need looking after."

"I'll walk back with her," said Lazlo "I'll make sure she's alright."

"We're not ready to go yet, anyway" interrupted Mitra.

"Aren't we?" asked Lazlo with a smile.

"No. We've got things to talk about."

Amir hid his surprise and amusement that Mitra wanted to make conversation with another human being. "OK, I'll go to find Mary." He turned away to conceal a smile.

When Amir went, Mitra turned to Lazlo. “I want to ask about your mother and father. Are they like Micheline and Pierre?”

“God, no! They are just as nice, but more serious. We’re Romanies and they have fun when we get together with our own, but their suffering is never far away. We came here in a leaky old boat when I was seven years old. I didn’t want to leave, and cried all the journey. But we weren’t liked and someone had burned our house down. It’s safer for us here.”

“I so wish I could live with parents. I lived with different families when my parents went to prison. I was always in the way, being shouted at and punished.”

“Punished?”

“Well I wasn’t very good. Actually, I was – er – what’s that word?”

“You mean naughty.”

“Yes, that’s it. I was naughty. At two houses I was raped. They said it was to make me behave. I only found out years later that’s what it’s called. It didn’t work anyway. Next day, I would throw things around and smash them. I was mean to the family’s own children because they weren’t treated like me. Then I’d be sent somewhere else.”

Lazlo put a comforting arm around her. “My parents are good people. They’re kind. You must come and meet them. They’re not jolly like Paul’s parents, but you’ll be welcomed.”

“Did you go to school here? I wanted to, but they said I was older. I was fourteen and they said I was eighteen and I had no papers. I’d torn them up. Did you like school?”

“Yes, I went to school and I met lots of friends. That’s where I met Paul. We both left school last summer.”

“You were lucky, having parents, going to school, and coming home to be looked after.”

Lazlo smiled. He’d never thought of himself as lucky before. “At least, there’s no one to boss you around,” he answered. “My parents are good, but they’re very old fashioned. They treat me like a child, but I’m sixteen. But they care about me.”

"Nobody cares about me," Mitra answered wistfully.

"I do. I think you're nice."

They sat in the square for a while, chatting of nothing in particular. Then cold and hunger made them move on. Lazlo walked up to Mitra's house.

"See you at club!" he called cheerfully as he set off for home. Amir and Mary were watching television when Mitra walked in.

"Have you enjoyed yourself? You were out a long time," asked Mary.

"Mm, it was alright," was the only reply.

Mary smiled and cast a knowing glance across at Amir but said nothing more.

Chapter Twelve

Lazlo and Paul became welcome visitors to the home. They called round to invite Mitra to the park to play football or to walk round the town centre. Sometimes they would all sit in Mitra's tiny room listening and singing along to Paul's radio. Despite the racket, it was a relief to Mary and Giselle that she had company and exercise instead of sprawling on the settee all day. Giselle, normally serene and wise, became animated when Paul was in the house, chatting to him in Lingala about mutual friends from the church they both attended. The priest was Congolese, so there was always a large percentage of people from the Congo in that congregation. As well as a place of worship, the church offered social interaction and inclusion, and endless gossip.

Somehow, the English group continued with a free lunch, although the contributions Mary received were becoming less and less. Flora, the lady whose efforts had provided the money in the first place, was finding it more difficult to source small grants to keep them going. Mary, Giselle and Amir all put one pound into the pot every week. Instead of taking turns to cook, Amir took on the task. After his successful Christmas dinner, he found he enjoyed the challenge of making a nutritious meal out of cheap ingredients. Paul joined the youth club and set off every Friday with Mitra and Lazlo and Amir and Mary followed behind. There was some routine to the week.

The housemates began to settle down to their daily life, although homesickness attacked them when they least expected it, producing a yearning, not for the unsafety of life they left behind, but for the people and land they loved. But there were things to do which made the present bearable. That is, for everyone except Hafida, who remained curled up on the living room floor by day and sobbing in her bedroom at night.

Mary felt guilty that she hadn't helped to improve Hafida's problems after almost a year of living with her. The others seemed to be resigned to the situation. Whenever Mary discussed it, they told her of the efforts they went to before Mary arrived. All forms of comfort, interest and gentle coaxing on Giselle's part, had no effect. Mitra's brusque and direct questions didn't seem to upset her, but neither did they provoke a reaction.

Some weeks earlier, the housemates had summoned a doctor and luckily it was a woman who answered the call. Hafida allowed herself to be examined and the doctor took a blood sample. A fortnight later a letter came to say all physical tests were normal, except that she was malnourished. A prescription for antidepressants and a diet advice leaflet was attached to the letter. The results and medication was explained to Hafida, who was completely unemotional. She took the prescription, but Giselle found it in the bin, covered in wet tea bags a few days later.

But Mary couldn't give up, and mentioned her concerns to William, the support worker from immigration when he came round to carry out his inspection of the property.

"Not really my problem unless she asks herself. I like a quiet life. This house doesn't give me any trouble. You girls tend to get on with it. Even Mitra's stopped yelling at me every time she sees me. You should hear what I put up with in a men's HMO." He shrugged his shoulders dismissively, but nevertheless, Mary noticed he wrote something on his clipboard.

A few days later, a letter arrived for Hafida. Mitra translated it whilst Hafida lay on the carpet in her penance position. Giselle and Mary were curious to know what it said.

"Oh, it's an appointment for counselling from Victims of Torture. It's hard to get one. There's a waiting list. Some of my friends have needed it, but they couldn't get in. Shame they didn't as she says she's not going. They're asking that someone goes with her."

"Mitra, please tell her I'll go with her!" Mary was anxious that Hafida would decline the only offer of help she'd received.

Mitra turned back to Hafida and delivered the message. Hafida made no reply, but got up and went to her room. Mary was not about to give up so easily. "Tell me the details and I'll remind her at the time," she asked Mitra.

Mitra handed over the letter. "You try. We can't do anything with her."

Mary took the letter for safekeeping, determined to make a difference to Hafida's life. Surely it could do no harm. It was worth a try to persuade her.

Meanwhile, Mitra had a request of her own. "Lazlo wants me to meet his parents. It's his birthday next week and he's having a special tea, and I'm invited. Can you come with me? I don't want to go on my own."

Mary was flattered and heartened by this invitation. "Let me see the date of the counselling. If I can, I'll go if I'm invited."

The party turned out to be the day before Hafida's appointment, which fitted in. Apart from the groups the friends attended, other commitments were rare. Mary felt she had a full, busy week at last, although it was nothing like the useful life she led at home.

"Can Amir come? I'll feel better with him around. I could get him to make a cake. He's becoming something of a chef these days."

"Mm, suppose so. Actually, Lazlo did say Amir as well."

This was something to look forward to. Amir happily made a cake in the shape of a number seventeen in English and Mary put on a pretty dress she'd bought from the charity shop months ago. This was the first occasion to wear it. She noticed that Mitra changed into a lovely off the shoulder top and her best jeans as soon as she saw Mary's outfit. It was very unusual to see Mitra in anything other than t shirts or jumpers.

They set off together, Mitra leading the way. Mary was surprised to find that Lazlo's house was quite near their own. It was only a ten-minute walk. The street was similar to theirs, with two rows of small terraced houses on either side of a narrow roadway, almost filled with parked cars. A tall, well-built man was waiting in the doorway, smiling a greeting. His fresh, young face looked so like Lazlo's that Mary immediately assumed it was his brother, until the man spoke.

"Hi, I'm Lazlo's father. Thank you for coming to see us."

"Father! I was sure it was er.... You look so young," she finished lamely, aware that she was being slightly rude.

He noticed her discomfort, and tried to reassure her. "Don't worry. It's alright. In my culture we marry very young. My wife and I have one precious child. Our Lazlo." He held out his hand. "I'm Otto. Do come in."

"Mary, and this is Amir. I assume you've met Mitra?"

"Yes, we've met." Otto smiled down at Mitra and turned to lead them into the house. Mary was startled to find his hair was pulled into a ponytail. It was longer than she remembered, but there was no mistaking that view from the back of his cap which she had watched every morning for weeks on end, when she first came to England. The broad, slightly hunched shoulders, the way he held himself, and his walk were all reminders of how his presence in the street gave her hope that life out there was somehow normal and ordinary. She hadn't ever expected to meet him. It was almost like meeting a film star.

She couldn't take her eyes off him, and stared silently until it almost became offensive. Embarrassed, she turned her attention to the house, which was small and modestly furnished, but cosy and welcoming. Otto's wife took the cake as she introduced herself.

"Hi, I am Agneska. Thank you for coming." Her Polish accent was stronger than Otto's and she seemed less confident. Slim, clear-skinned and pretty, with a mane of dark brown hair, she, too looked even more like a sibling of Lazlo's than a parent. Paul and his parents were already in the living room.

"HI, this is my mum, my dad and my girlfriend, Cerise," said Paul proudly as they walked in.

"Pleased to meet you. I've heard all about you from Mitra. I'll get you both a beer. My Dad gave me some," said Cerise. She was charming and self-assured and appeared perfectly at ease in Lazlo's house. Mary realised the surprise she was feeling was showing on her face when Paul's mother said, "She's a good hostess, yes? We love her. She will make a good wife one day."

"Not one day soon!" retorted Cerise. "I've got lots of things to do before then." She was slim and pretty and had the same lively face and smooth dark skin as Paul. She was dressed in bright colours and a pair of huge golden earrings dangled from her ears.

"Do you work round here?" Mary said to Otto once they were seated in the living room. "We live on Nelson Street and I used to watch you walking down the road every morning when I first came to this country. I was so lonely. I felt as if I knew you."

"Really?" Otto answered. "I leave at six most mornings. I have a cleaning job at a factory. I don't see many people. They're all still in bed."

"So was I but I couldn't sleep. I dreamt about my mother every night. I could cope in the day, but once in bed, it all came back to me."

"I know how that feels. When my parents died, we were forced out of our home in Poland. We lived in tents and caves until we came here. We travelled in cars until we got to Calais, then took an open boat across the channel with twenty other people. We landed in Dover and asked for asylum because of the treatment we received. It's not necessary to do that now. When Poland joined the European Union we were allowed to stay, but we had to pay for our papers. I was not allowed to work until then, so we had no money."

"So how did you manage?"

"I was lucky. I had a friend in my landlord. He didn't mind that we were Romanies. We were given this house when we first asked for asylum. We've lived here ever since we came to England. It was very, how you say, broken. I mended it with things I found on the tip. He asked me to mend other houses he rented. When I was allowed to work he gave me a job. But I also need my cleaning job."

"Did he pay you for the work you'd done before?"

"No, but he let me stay here, rent free, until I got the money for us. Some people had relatives to borrow from, and some took loans that took years to pay. We are our own people now."

He seemed to Mary to be such a nice man. He was obviously being exploited by this landlord, who, it seemed, wasn't paying very much for his work on the rented houses, but compared to his Romany friends he was very fortunate. It seemed strange, almost surreal, to be sitting talking with this man after she'd spent so long wondering about him from afar.

Lazlo's family proved to be excellent hosts. Agneska's food was delicious and consisted of lots of homemade savouries she'd spent all day preparing. There were tiny, crescent shaped pies with an assortment of fillings, strongly flavoured sausages, dumplings and little cups full of beetroot soup. Amir's seventeen shaped cake was quickly demolished to a few crumbs.

The atmosphere was so welcoming that everyone was put at ease immediately. Otto managed to get all his guests dancing Romany reels until they were exhausted. Then he sang some traditional songs with Agneska, much to the embarrassment of Lazlo, who hid his face in a cushion. However, no one else had anything but praise for the singing. Mary cast a maternal glance across at Mitra, who was already quite boisterous, when Otto produced a bottle of vodka. He saw her concern and winked reassuringly. "Mary, I have only the one bottle. I have been saving it for a special occasion. I can't afford more. One drink each, for the young people?"

"Yes, of course!" Mary was touched that she was being treated as a worried parent. Neither Mitra nor Otto needed her permission to do anything, but it felt like having a family again, being included in decisions. A small glass was handed round to each person. Even Amir took one and raised it to Lazlo's health.

All too soon, it was time to wander home. Paul, his parents and Cerise set off in the opposite direction. Mary began to feel a little anxious about Hafida. Giselle had stayed behind to be with her, although she would have greatly enjoyed the party. Hafida's behaviour hadn't changed but her appearance had. Always a slim person, she was now so drawn that her eyes and cheeks were sunken.

Mitra's voice broke into her thoughts. "I might have a party for my birthday. I'll be sixteen soon. I didn't even tell anybody when I turned fifteen."

"Why not?" Mary asked. "We would have liked to know."

"Well, I'm nineteen now, according to immigration. They wouldn't listen to me. On my arc card my birthday is January the first. I was furious, but then I forgot all about it."

"We'll spoil you on your real birthday, this time. Won't we, Amir?"

"Yes, of course!" he answered. "You can have a cake too, and friends round."

Mitra laughed, delighted at the thought. Her pleasure took Mary's mind off Hafida for the rest of the journey. "It will be good to this again. I'm so glad you enjoyed it, Mitra."

Amir went back to his flat as he had someone from the housing office coming the next morning. Mary lay in bed, wondering about the task she'd set herself for the next day. She'd promised the others she would take Hafida to the counsellor. It wasn't something she was looking forward to and she slept badly that night, despite the lovely evening spent at the party. She dreaded what could be uncovered during the visit, how Hafida would react, or whether she'd consent to go at all.

At six o'clock she found herself staring out of the window, watching until Otto came into view, walking along, shoulders hunched and ponytail swinging from back of his cap, to let her know that this was just another day. The sight of him brought back memories of her first morning in England, when, a year ago, she stood, grief stricken and friendless on this very spot, a week after burying her murdered mother. But life was better now. She had friends, she had things to do, and she had Amir. Soon, she would have her daughter back.

She watched Otto go down the street until he was just a speck, recognisable as a person only because the speck was moving. He had been a sign of normality in that difficult time. Then she drew a deep breath and got on with the day.

Chapter Thirteen

To Mary's surprise, Hafida was willing to go to the counselling session and even said a whispered "thank you" when Mitra translated that Mary had offered to go with her. They sat together on the bus, without touching each other. Even so, Mary could feel Hafida's slight body trembling beside her.

They were met by two kindly middle-aged ladies, who introduced themselves. One was the counsellor, the other the interpreter. Hafida was shown into a small room containing three chairs placed in a semicircle. Mary watched Hafida as she was guided to a seat, then the door was closed.

After what seemed like days, but was actually a couple of hours, Hafida emerged again. The ladies were composed, but both had tears in their eyes. Hafida's harsh, rasping sobs shook her frail body like a rag doll. An appointment was given for the following week. Mary took the card and offered her free hand to Hafida. She was pleased to find that she took it and leaned against her for comfort.

On the bus home, she clung to Mary's arm, and managed to whisper "Thank you" a second time. Once in the house, she went straight to her room. Mitra took up a cup of tea, then left her undisturbed. Giselle was making the evening meal when Hafida walked into the room and sat down at the table. She looked anxiously at the other women, who smiled back, trying not to make a big deal of it. But this was the first time she'd joined them for a meal, with the exception of Christmas Day.

It had been a harrowing experience for Mary. The fact that there was some improvement in Hafida's life, however small, made the whole experience worthwhile. But the distress she'd witnessed brought painful reminders of her first few days in this country. She tried to think of pleasant things, like the party the day before. She knew it was selfish, but she really didn't want to go again to the next appointment. She discussed her feelings with Amir when she slept at his flat a couple of days later.

"I feel it's better if the same person goes each time, but I just can't bring myself to offer. And the counsellor wants someone with her when she comes out. It's so upsetting and it's making me relive lots of awful times."

"I understand. But you are such a good person that I know you will do it. And I am here to help you."

Mary smiled. He always knew what to say. "You have such faith in me. More than I have in myself. It's the day after tomorrow. I've not recovered from last time yet."

"You will face it. It will be, how you say, ok? And not as bad as the first one."

Amir was right. The two ladies met Hafida and shepherded her into the same room as last time. Mary took a book into the waiting room and managed to read it. When Hafida emerged, shaken and limp, she held a hand out to Mary and accepted her own appointment card from the counsellor. On the bus home she turned to Mary with a wan little smile on her face. Mary linked her arm and they sat in comfortable silence throughout the journey.

Each week saw a small improvement in Hafida's mood. She began to sit at the table at mealtimes and even spoke a few words in English to the housemates. She came with them to the post office to collect her allowance instead of waiting until it was almost closing time. She still lay, curled up on the carpet every day but the sessions were shorter each time. Mary continued to accompany her to the counsellor's and it became easier for both of them.

One day as Giselle was preparing vegetables in the kitchen, Hafida came in with a carrier bag full of food. No one had noticed that she'd gone out, but all presumed she was in her room.

"I will cook," she said hesitantly. "I have this." She showed Giselle the bag. Mitra and Mary looked on, astounded. Giselle said gently, "That would be lovely, Hafida. Thank you," and stood aside to let her put out the food. It was youth club night so Mary and Mitra disappeared upstairs to get ready.

"I'm not sure what this meal's going to be like. If we don't make food she lives off crisps and bananas," said Mitra as they mounted the stairs together. "It's risky."

"Well as you don't cook at all, it must be better than your attempts. Give her a chance."

"Humm!" was the only reply.

But soon a tempting aroma of spices and herbs floated up to the bathroom and Mitra poked her head round the door. "Save me some!" she yelled down to the kitchen. Mary, getting changed in her room, smiled to herself.

The meal was every bit as delicious as it smelled. Chicken pieces cooked with garlic, tomatoes, coriander and onions were the flavours Mary could identify, but there were other things in there she had never tasted before. She set off to youth club feeling elated that Hafida had come to life.

Lazlo and Paul were already at the club when Mary, Amir and Mitra arrived, and for the first time, Cerise accompanied them. They all ran up in a state of excitement.

"Rob has a new project! You're just the person for it!" Lazlo shook Mitra by the shoulders as he spoke. "You'll be great at it!"

"Let the girl get her coat off first," the vicar interrupted. "Then I can tell her myself."

Lazlo pulled off Mitra's coat, unable to wait.

"This is what's happening," Rob explained. "The sixth form college deputy head asked me to put on a workshop for the year twelve and thirteen pupils to talk about asylum seekers in the town. He asked me because he knows I have young people from different countries coming to the youth club."

"And you want me to do it?" said Mitra.

"It would sound much better to the children coming from someone near their own age," said Rob.

"She doesn't hesitate or play things down. She's truthful and her English is good." Lazlo said.

"I don't know if I want to do it. I'm not good in front of all those people."

"They're all just kids, like us," Lazlo explained. "They're not going to give you marks out of ten."
"I'll think about it. But why me?"
"Think about it, if you want, but if you get to see what goes on in there and meet the teachers, maybe, when you get leave to remain, they'll remember you and let you join the college."
"Huh! When will that be? I'll be an old woman before I get leave to remain," Mitra retorted. She ran off to join a group of young people round the pool table. Amir followed her and joined in the game. Mary could see him talking pleasantly and laughing with the teenagers, but couldn't hear any of the conversation. Mitra didn't seem to be taking any notice. However, after a few minutes, she came back and approached the vicar, who was talking to Mary. "Rob, what day is this college thing?"
"Every Friday morning for about four weeks, until the end of term," he replied. "I can take you, if you like."
"I want Mary to come with me. I'll go if she will."
"I'll have to ask Giselle if she can go with Hafida to counselling, but if she agrees, I'll come," Mary answered.
Rob smiled benignly at the two of them. "Well done, girls! I'll tell the head the workshop's on. I thought you weren't up for it."
"I've got plenty to say," Mitra replied. "I just didn't know it until now."
Mary set off home, leaving Mitra to wander back with Lazlo, Paul and Cerise.
Once in the house, Mary lost no time in discussing the counselling sessions with Giselle.
"Bien sur, I don't mind. It will fill up my day. But it's Hafida who may not like the change. You must ask her first."
"I'm waiting for Mitra to translate to make sure she understands. She'll be home soon."
Mitra arrived home half an hour later, full of enthusiasm. "Lazlo thinks I'll be great at this school thing," she said as she threw herself on the settee. "I'd love to know what goes on in there."

"Can you explain to Hafida? On second thoughts, I'll speak and you translate. We must be gentle. She's come so far, we can't have any setbacks."

"I can be gentle!" Mitra retorted, but she was so excited that she went to the bottom of the stairs and yelled "Hafida" as loudly as she could. Poor Hafida came down, trembling, and peeped cautiously round the door.

"It's alright, it's nothing bad," Mary tried to reassure her. But a look at Hafida's stricken face told her that Hafida had only recognised the word 'bad'. Hastily she turned to Mitra. "Tell her that Giselle will be going with her on Friday and that she will look after her well and there's no need to be afraid."

Mitra relayed the message and Mary was relieved to see Hafida's face relax into a smile. "I can do that." She turned to Giselle. "Thank you."

Though the sessions with Hafida were becoming easier to bear, Mary was glad of a break from the stress. She felt slightly guilty at her relief that Giselle was taking over. She resolved to take on the task as soon as the college stuff finished. She was looking forward to being in a classroom again, among young people. This was where she was most at home. It also made her feel a little closer to Sara.

The following Friday found them at the college gates, gazing at a massive building with several entrances and a large forecourt milling with teenagers. Even Mitra's bravado was wavering as people walked past without noticing them, and disappeared into the various doors dotted round the building. They were standing there, unsure what to do next, when Lazlo appeared.

"HI! I'm glad I've not missed you!" He hugged them both. "Paul has friends who come here, and I've been to a few concerts with him. I'll show you where to go."

Gratefully they followed him to the secretary's office. As they approached, a charming young man rushed up to them and greeted them in a strong Northern Irish accent.

"I was just about to send out a search party of students. I would have met you at the gate, but I couldn't park and had to go round the back."

"How would you have known us among all these people?" said Mary.

"Probably by the look of confusion on your faces." He laughed. "Everyone gets lost here. I'm James. I'm teaching current affairs."

"I'm Mary and this is Mitra, your speaker, and her friend Lazlo. Lazlo and I are here for support."

He showed them into a large hall, twice as big as the church rooms they were used to. Rows and rows of chairs stretched around a screen which took up half the back wall. Mitra looked anxiously at Mary, who could tell she'd lost the cocky attitude she usually protected herself with.

"It will be fine," she reassured her.

"I know lots of them from hanging out with Paul," said Lazlo. They're ok."

Mitra managed a shrug. "Mm, suppose so."

At that moment the door opened and the students poured in, chattering, filling the chairs, swapping seats, and shouting across to one another until James called them to order. Lazlo and Mary sat in a corner of the room.

"This is Mitra," James announced when he had the attention of the class. "She's come to talk to you about being an asylum seeker. There's a lot of stories in the media about this, and I want you to hear what real people go through instead of believing everything you read. Over to you, Mitra."

After a quick glance at her friends, Mitra stepped forward. In perfect English, she described her life in Iran after her parents were imprisoned for political beliefs and her journey in distance, time and culture and her age dispute. The students were riveted. Even James was transfixed by her honest and hard-hitting account of her life. She finished her talk by saying, "I was fourteen when I came here. No one believed me. They said I was eighteen, so I never went to school. Children from other countries must go to school. They may not pass any exams, but that is where they will learn the language, how to behave, what life is like here. That will be their education. Please remember that when children come here."

"Well done, that was really interesting." James broke the stunned silence. "Any questions?"

Everyone stared at him for a few moments, then one brave soul put a hesitant hand in the air. "Were you cold? Was it winter when you came?"

"Perhaps Mitra's friends could join in at this point," said James.

Mary and Lazlo looked at each other. "Go on!" Lazlo whispered to Mary. "I can tell you want to." Mary got up and indicated to Lazlo to follow, and with a sigh, he did so.

"My name is Mary and I come from Zimbabwe and it was very cold the day I arrived in this country. I hated the cold weather and I'm still not used to it. In Zimbabwe we can predict it, but here, every day is different."

"I am Lazlo, and my country is worse than here in the winter. I am from Poland but I've been here since I was seven, so it's hard to remember. My parents tell stories about snowy winters in their childhood and having to sleep in a cow shed."

As unobtrusively as possible, Mary tried to support Mitra and Lazlo if the questions got too difficult or upsetting.

"How did you manage without your parents?" asked a girl about Mitra's age.

"Oh, I can look after myself," said Mitra, airily.

"But don't you miss having someone to do things, like washing up and cooking?"

For a moment, Mitra hesitated to reply, and Mary caught sight of her expression of regret.

"Other relatives and friends looked after me when I was a child," Mary interrupted. "My mother was busy saving the world. Was it the same for you, Mitra?"

Mitra glanced across and nodded gratefully.

"What about food? Did you like fish and chips and burgers?"

"I hated them at first, but now I love them," answered Mitra, and Lazlo agreed heartily.

"Lazlo, what did you learn about England, before you came?" asked a boy.

"I only went to school when I came here," Lazlo answered. "We moved around a lot in Poland, because we were Romanies. We never settled anywhere."

"Did you live in a caravan?"

"No, mostly caves and sheds but sometimes houses."

"I bet that was ace!"

"I only remember being cold and hungry, especially at night."

"Moving around must have been good," the boy persisted.

"We only moved when somebody beat up my Dad." Lazlo's face changed at the memory and Mary hastily jumped in with, "I moved around a lot, too, but mostly in the same big town."

Skilfully, Mary guided the workshop without compromising the flow of ideas coming from both the students and the visitors.

The weather had opened up a discussion and proved to be a social and cultural leveller. The metaphorical and imagined ice was broken. The young people carried on eagerly asking question after question until James called a halt by raising his hands in the air. There was complete silence for a few moments. Then James began to clap. The students, having had permission by his actions, joined in and soon were whooping their approval. Mitra shot a delighted glance at Mary and Lazlo. James called for peace a second time, then signalled to the students that the session was over. They filed out, chattering to each other.

"I really enjoyed listening to that and it reminded me of when I first came to England from Northern Ireland and the problems I'd forgotten about until now. Thank you, Mitra, Mary and Lazlo for a very informative morning."

"I really enjoyed it," said Mary. "I was a teacher at home. I miss it so much."

"I have three more Fridays if you're all free. They've learned so much social history and geography in one lesson that I'd love to continue. I've already got ideas for teaching in between your talks, to add to them. And thank you, Mary, for handling it so well."

"I love to be around young people. I miss my daughter who's back home. She's safe there, but I'd love her to be here, with me."

"Is that why you came?"

"I only came to keep Mitra company. I didn't think you'd notice," said Mary. "But I was hoping to be asked back."

"I'll be here next week." Said Mitra, casually. Mary smiled, but said nothing more.

"I'll do it if I'm not working with my Dad," said Lazlo. "He's training me to repair houses, so I might be busy."

James showed them out through vast corridors filled with teenagers milling around, enjoying their lunch break. The trio set off home, looking forward to the next time.

Chapter Fourteen

After she was attacked, Sara changed schools on Auntie Toto's advice. It was a pleasant, caring little place, tucked away among poorer houses in the district. Her uniform was completely different to the one for her previous school. There she wore a red shirt and black skirt. The new uniform was grey, which disguised her a little and gave her some protection. Academically, however, the school fell far short, making lessons boring. Most of the things she was taught had already been covered in the old school. But she felt safe there, which mattered most. The rape was the worst experience of her young life. Auntie was kind and supportive, but Sara missed her mother so much. Her Amia could do anything and had a solution to every problem. Life went on in that little village. She made friends, went to church, helped Auntie with the chores and weeks there turned into months. She was patient, but she never settled. Everything was on hold.

Her best friend was called Ruth. They met soon after Sara started at school. Ruth saw her standing outside the classroom one morning. It was very early and none of the teachers had yet arrived. Sara looked around, not knowing what to do. In the end, she sat on the door step, feeling and looking conspicuous. Ruth was the next person to arrive.

"Hi, you're the new girl, aren't you?"

It was nice to see a friendly face, but past experiences made Sara shy and cautious. Every day was a challenge of unfamiliar people and places. She nodded but didn't make any attempt at conversation. Undeterred, Ruth sat down beside her.

"I felt like this when I got here." Ruth's voice was comforting and soothing. "You'll find everyone is ok. My last school had lots of bullies but here, people get on with each other."

“Where did you come from?” Sara ventured to ask, still a little apprehensive.

“We lived near the centre of Harare. There were lots of riots and my Amia didn’t think it was safe. She moved us here to be near my uncle .He works on a farm round here. I’ve no father and she thought we needed a man to protect us.”

Sara felt that this person understood her. “I haven’t got a father either,” she confided. “I live with my aunty. My father ran off soon after I was born.”

“Why did he do that?”

“He upset somebody in the government. I don’t know how.”

Immediately she said it, Sara realised it might not be a good idea to tell people such things. But Ruth smiled and said reassuringly, “He might come back one day.”

Sara didn’t answer. However, she felt that this person could be trusted and no other questions were asked. After that meeting, they sought each other out to share homework, books, clothes, gossip or simply enjoy the company. Sara never mentioned the attack and gradually it receded to the back of her mind, not forgotten but slightly less important than before.

Then, one day, the two girls were sitting on the grass outside the school door, eating maize cakes for lunch. Ruth noticed a boy from their class looking at them.

“What’s wrong? Do you want some?” She held out a piece of cake for him.

He ignored her and addressed Sara. “Did your Amia make that?”

Before Sara could answer, Ruth said, “She lives with her Auntie.”

The boy smiled and wandered off. Neither Ruth nor Sara thought about the boy again, but Sara felt a pang of loneliness at the mention of her mother. She missed her all the time, but some days were worse than others.

So when Auntie said it was time to send her to England instead of waiting, she was overjoyed. Auntie didn’t say why she’d come to this decision. Until now, they were expecting Sara would be sent for. But no explanation was given and Sara accepted the news without question, being told that it would be better to go immediately. Sara trusted her judgement, and looked forward to seeing her Amia again. It seemed like a great adventure.

Auntie Toto explained that she had arranged that she would go and live as a house guest with a family friend. The lodgings would be in return for some help with the children. Leaving her house had never been mentioned before. Auntie simply got on with life from day to day and didn't ever complain. For the first time, it occurred to Sara that Auntie might be in danger because she was staying with her. There was never a sense of fear or anger in the home. This was something Sara had taken for granted, until now. Auntie must know something to have made so many arrangements. But she was too young to realise how much her father's sister had given up to keep her niece alive.

When that night, some people tried to break into their little house, they were both terrified. It was sheer good luck that neither of them were in the outside toilet at the time or they would almost certainly have been killed. They were both fast asleep when suddenly, loud bangs awoke their slumbers. At first it was hard to realise what was happening. But then, a slim shaft of light appeared through the darkness and lit up part of the door frame.

"Someone's breaking the door down!" Auntie Toto was up, alert and shaking a confused Sara out of sleep. "Get up and help me!"

There was only one entrance to their home, and Auntie was quick to push all their furniture against it. They sat shivering on the floor in the middle of the room, clinging to each other.

It wasn't cold, but Sara's teeth were chattering with fear. She wanted to die and get it over with, before they came in and she had to endure the pain of the last attack. The battering seemed to go on all night but Auntie said it only lasted about an hour. They heard shouting and swearing along with the blows, but the voices weren't any they recognised. It was difficult to know how many there were. Finally, an argument started and the attackers went away. Auntie and Sara had no idea who their saviours were, but someone had been brave enough to stop the raiders. Footsteps got fainter, voices faded away and at last there was silence.

Sleep was impossible after that. Auntie Toto held on to Sara's shaking body until daylight. They spent the rest of the night listening for movements or strange voices. The next day they stood outside their house, feeling exhausted after the effort of clearing the doorway by pushing the piled up beds, chairs and tables away, which had formed a barrier to protect them against their cruel invaders. Once out, they knew they couldn't go back in. Hanging around the village would be far too dangerous.

Their neighbours were sympathetic and helped all they could, but Sara's presence in the community was putting them all in danger and they were relieved that she was leaving. Auntie Toto needed to get rid of all her stuff. No one had much furniture in their houses but at such short notice it was difficult to find buyers for their humble things. People offered goods instead of money if that was all they had.

They managed to sell, exchange or give away all their belongings except the clothes they were wearing. People gave what they could afford which in most cases wasn't much. Some small items were exchanged for water carriers and food for the journey. One woman gave Sara a bag which could be worn next to the body round the waist and some silver money with the Queen of England's head on it. Inside the bare little house, friends and neighbours said tearful goodbyes, leaving at intervals so as not to attract attention.

They were ready to leave by midday. Sara put on her school uniform and she walked along with a group of girls all dressed like her, pretending to go to school after the lunch break. Her grey blouse and skirt helped her fade into the background. Her school bag was on her back as usual, but instead of books, it contained food and her only set of clean underclothes. The little bag was around her waist, tucked under her skirt. Auntie Toto followed behind, wrapped in a dark shawl, her face partially covered.

When the other girls went into class, Auntie flagged down a car and, after some haggling, paid the driver to take them to the next town. It was more expensive than usual, but they couldn't afford to attract attention by standing in the street. Neither of them spoke during the journey. Sara held on to Auntie's hand, suddenly aware of the ordeal she was facing alone, and Auntie's own predicament.

When they left the car, Sara's fears escalated. She spoke for the first time since they left the house. "What will you do, where will you go? I'm scared for you, Auntie. Your friends don't even know you're coming today."

"I won't need to tell them," Auntie replied. "They begged me to stay with them to help with the children. I know they'll take me in. They're really worried about me."

"Have you spoken to them? When did you last see them?"

"I saw them a few days ago. They're old friends. They can be trusted. I was warned this might happen. Someone recognised you. I didn't want to frighten you, but I got ready to run."

"Why didn't you tell me? I had no idea."

"I wanted our last few days to be happy. I didn't know how long a time we had together. It turned out to be much less than I thought."

"I'll miss you, Auntie. I don't want to go on my own."

"You'll be fine. There isn't enough money for us both to go. And maybe I'll get to come and see you, once you're over there."

Sara was silent again. She was afraid of the immediate future. She never imagined going to her mother would be like this. Panic gripped her stomach and turned it over and over and over. But she remembered how frightened she had been last night. Whatever happened, surely it couldn't be worse.

The taxi came to a halt on a busy street. "Alright here?" said the driver.

"Yes, that's fine."

Auntie handed him the fare and he drove off, leaving them standing in a strange town with people bustling around them, dodging heavy traffic as it crawled along the road. The noise and activity reminded Sara of her old home in Harare which she'd shared with her mother and grandmother in what now seemed a lifetime ago. At least, here they could get lost in the crowd without being recognised.

"We need to find someone called Yusuf," Auntie said, looking up and down the street. "I think he's around here somewhere. I was told it was a black door with gold writing."

It took a lot of walking past doors, but eventually they realised that a battered, mud spattered piece of wood looking more like an old gate had a gold paper number three stuck on it with tape.

Tentatively, Auntie knocked on it. A tall Asian man with a thin, bearded face and long hair straggling to his shoulders opened it and stared at them for a few seconds.

"Well?" he said at last.

"I'm looking for Yusuf." Auntie's voice had a tremor in it.

"Name?"

"Toto."

Without speaking further, the man stepped aside and gestured them to come in. The room was as dingy within as it was outside. He pointed to two rusty metal chairs. As they sat down, he demanded "Where's the money?"

"Here." Auntie opened her shawl to reveal a bag hung round her neck. It was filled with banknotes.

"Zim dollars not worth much. Worth less and less each day. Give me those as well." He pointed to four bangles on Auntie's wrist. They were made of gold. Sara had never seen Auntie take them off before. Without hesitation she removed them and handed them over. "Any more?"

Sara opened her schoolbag and took out the money Auntie had given her for the journey. Yusuf snatched it and stuffed it away with the rest.

"Which one's going? There only enough here for one."

"Sara, my niece."

He picked up a mobile phone and disappeared through a door in the back of the room. Sara clung tightly to Auntie Toto's arm. Waves of nausea rose from her stomach.

"You'll be alright. It will be an adventure." Auntie stroked her head. "You're going to join your Amia. I will miss you. You're all I have left of my little brother. I promised him that I'd look out for you."

"I wish you were coming, Auntie."

"I'll be fine here. Nobody knows us. My friend lives in this town. I'll write as soon as I can. I know the address in England. I didn't dare write it down, it's not safe. People are still trying to find your grandmother's supporters. But I memorised it."

At that moment, Yusuf returned and ushered them out. A car was waiting outside the door. Sara gave Toto one last hug. "I don't want to leave you, Auntie."

"I think my brother is in heaven. I don't want his little girl to join him just yet. I want her to go to England. "

The car door opened and the driver beckoned Sara into the back seat. As they drove off, she watched through the back window until Auntie disappeared among the crowds of people milling about the street. She turned around and closed her eyes in an attempt to shut out the fear. But she was back in the house in the dark, watching the gap in the door frame growing larger and larger as the intruders battered away outside.

Chapter Fifteen

Rob was delighted to hear how well the workshop had gone when the friends turned up at youth club that evening. Paul and Cerise were curious enough to want to tag along on one of the sessions.

"I don't think James will mind. He was pleased with the reaction we got," Mary said. "I might suggest that we split into groups for question time so everyone gets a chance to speak to us."

"There's the teacher in you, coming out," laughed Rob. "He might tell you to mind your own business, in a polite way, of course."

"There could be a few racists in there who want to get their point across without the teacher's knowledge," answered Mary. "But I can deal with them."

"But can the others?" The vicar was sceptical.

"I can help them. Anyway, James can say no if he needs more control."

"Yes, I suppose so."

"Some subjects are sensitive and I realised I could protect Mitra and Lazlo from overwhelming memories. Without being too obvious, of course."

"I can see you were quite an asset," Rob replied.

Amir didn't join in the conversation until he and Mary got home. The teenagers went ahead of them and piled into Mitra's tiny room to play their favourite CDs for Paul and Cerise.

"You must be careful what you say to people. You don't know what the students' parents are like," Amir warned Mary, once they were alone in the living room.

"I can handle students, and Mitra can definitely stick up for herself."

"If that means she can defend herself, then I agree. But I will come with you next time."

"I love teaching, especially teenagers. It's what I do best. If they're prejudiced, I can open their minds. I don't need a chaperone."

"What's a chaperone?"

"Never mind."

"You're not their teacher, though, are you? James is the teacher and he only asked for Mitra, not you."

Mary was about to reply when Giselle walked in. "Hallo, you two! I'm pleased to say it went well with Hafida this morning."

Mary felt a little ashamed. With all the excitement of the workshop, she'd forgotten all about Hafida and her counselling.

"She came home and cooked a meal before she went to her room." Giselle pointed to the oven. "It's in there, if you want some. She's obviously feeling better."

The subject of the college was dropped and Mary warmed up the remains of the prepared meal and added some rice so that they could all share some of Hafida's efforts.

Lazlo, Paul and Cerise headed home. Amir stayed the night, but didn't mention the college students again. But Mary was determined to have her say at the class the next week. She had never felt so elated and so useful during her time in England. The English classes for their adult friends were enjoyable, but this was so much more stimulating. She slept dreamlessly that night and woke thinking about the students. For the first time, she didn't start the day with thoughts of her dead mother.

The following week Mary turned up with three more people than last time, feeling confident that James, the teacher would be agreeable to her lesson plan and ideas. Paul and Cerise were keen to find out what was going on. Amir simply went to stop Mary from taking over completely.

"Please don't tell the teacher what to do," he implored as they walked through the college grounds to the entrance.

"I shall be very tactful," Mary answered calmly.

"Tactful?"

"It means making him think it was his idea all along."

"How can you do that when only one person was invited, and it wasn't you?"

Mary smiled but didn't bother to reply. James met them at the door, taken aback by the numbers of people who entered the hall.

"I hope you don't mind," Mary said in her sweetest voice, "but some friends are really interested in the lessons last week. Could they observe quietly, from the back?"

"Of course." James turned to Paul and Cerise. "Welcome. Where are you from?"

"We're both from the Congo, but we met here, at the Catholic Church," Paul replied, taking Cerise's hand as he said it.

"Would you be willing to say a few words to the students? Mitra and Lazlo did so well last week. Because they are a similar age, the students were really impressed. It was so much easier for them to empathise. I based two more lessons on the subjects we discussed last week."

"Yes, we'd love to!" Paul answered and Cerise nodded enthusiastically in agreement.

"There might not be much time left for questions if everyone speaks," said Mary. "I'd like everyone to have a turn, however briefly."

"Perhaps we could split into three groups after everyone has told their story," said James. "Then the students could ask questions to two people and all students get a chance to ask before the break. I'll supervise the students closely. I promise."

Mary avoided Amir's eye. "Mm, that might work." She smiled at James as if he'd come up with a brilliant idea.

The session went really well. The students were more comfortable with the whole process and interacted perfectly. Even Amir enjoyed it. His and Mary's group were curious, polite and respectful. When the class filed out, Amir noticed one boy had a mobile phone out as if he was going to take a picture.

"Please don't take my photo, it's not my best day," he joked. The boy stuffed his phone in his pocket immediately, but Amir felt slightly uneasy. Once at home, he mentioned it to Mary.

"He didn't take a photo, but I thought it is dangerous let people we don't know to have such information."

"I agree. He probably just admires you, but we won't take the risk. I'll tell James about it. He can warn the whole class against it without identifying the person. The rest of us can't tell him who it is because we don't know the children by name."

"Keep an eye on them."

"I will. Trust me."

Amir didn't answer. Although he enjoyed the sessions in college, he wasn't as keen as Mary, who came to life and blossomed in the teaching environment. She seemed capable of handling any situation. He had to trust her judgement and capabilities. He worried about her, but respected her wishes and said no more. Soon, the whole incident was pushed to the back of his mind.

As it happened, there were no expressions of hostility or racism from the teenagers. Friday morning went well, and James thanked them all profusely for their time and efforts.

"I hope you realise what a difference it's made to the students. Meeting real asylum seekers has shown them that they are ordinary people and has helped dispel the myths that are around at the moment. If they can spread the message to their friends and families that there are good, bad and indifferent refugees, just like any other community, it has been worthwhile."

"I would love to come to this college!" said Mitra as James was showing them out. "I'm sorry next week will be the last session."

"Well, ask me how to apply when you get leave to remain and I'll see what I can do."

"Me too!" said Cerise. "I'm hoping I'll still be young enough when I'm allowed to stay."

"I hope so, too. You're both ambitious and intelligent, and that's the kind of person who does well here. Good luck." He winked at them and waved as they went on their way.

“He is a really nice man,” Cerise observed. “Not like the teachers I had in the Congo.”

“I never went to school for more than a few days,” Mitra answered. “I was moved around so much between relatives’ houses that in the end, I just wasn’t learning anything, so I stopped going. Then when I came here, they said I was eighteen and too old.”

“Who taught you to speak English so well?” asked Paul.

“I taught myself, by watching television, and using the computers in the library. I wanted to know what people were saying about me, and why I was supposed to be older.”

Lazlo put a comforting arm round Mitra’s shoulders. “I bet you’re really clever, Mitra. I bet you learn loads when you get to college.”

Mitra didn’t reply, but simply snuggled closer to him.

When they returned, Giselle and Hafida were still at the counsellor’s. The previous day, resourceful Amir had brought bread, hummus and salad in large quantities for lunch. Mary and the young people were busy enjoying the food when they were joined by the other two housemates.

“Did it go well?” asked Mary as they walked in. “There’s enough here for you to share.” She indicated the large loaves that were quickly being demolished by the teenagers. “Amir bought all this bread yesterday just as the baker’s was closing.”

Giselle sat down at the table. “Mm I’m very hungry,” she said, taking a hunk of bread. Hafida sat down beside her. ”Mm, I’m hungry,” she repeated.

Everyone looked up and smiled. Hafida had come a long way in a few weeks.

Chapter Sixteen

When the last Friday of the sessions came to an end, James had a little surprise for his visitors. One of the girls presented them with a bouquet of spring flowers. Deep red tulips and orange cupped daffodils had been picked from the college garden that morning, by the students. It was a simple gesture, but one which was very much appreciated.

"We are so often criticised as spongers and layabouts that it's nice when someone values us. People think we come here for the benefits," Lazlo told James, as he gathered round with the others to admire the gift.

"They will have pride of place at our home," said Mary.

"Lazlo, Paul and Cerise are always in my room, listening to music," added Mitra. "I'll put some in there for us to look at."

"Don't forget, if you have a chance to study here, we'll help if we can," James called after them as they went on their way.

Giselle and Hafida came in soon after the others, and Amir served up the bread and smoked fish he'd bought the evening before.

"I think we'll have to let you do all the shopping," said Giselle admiringly. "At home, men never shop for food."

"He has an eye for a bargain," said Mary.

"A bargain?" Amir shot a puzzled glance at the women.

"Never mind."

"Small money?" offered Hafida. "Like that?" She held up her hand to show a tiny gap between thumb and forefinger.

"You're doing so well! That's right!" Mary was genuinely thrilled to hear Hafida join in a conversation.

Later that day Mary asked Giselle how the counselling mornings were going. "I'll be willing to go back to accompanying Hafida if you want me to."

“It’s fine, Mary. We’re used to each other now. Although she hasn’t told me anything of her past, she is much calmer. I wouldn’t like to change her routine again.”

Mary’s offer was genuine, but she couldn’t help feeling relieved. Hafida’s distress on those first visits made Mary’s own memories much harder to bear. She scolded herself for being such a coward, but her mother’s death floated around her brain, sometimes strongly, sometimes fainter, but never absent. She reminded herself that she was lucky to be here and that her daughter was safe in a village, out of harm’s way, until she could send for her. She was very careful not to mention Sara’s whereabouts, even among friends, in case they inadvertently mentioned it in earshot of someone who might jeopardise Sara’s safety. Toto knew Mary’s address but promised never to write it down in case it got into the wrong hands. No news from Zimbabwe meant good news. Her daughter might be bored and lonely, but she was safe.

The next morning, William, the immigration support worker, paid his routine visit to the house. “Any problems, girls?” he said cheerfully, while writing on a clipboard.

“Not today,” answered Mitra. “Well, actually, there’s lots of things but you won’t do anything about them.” His visits always put her in a bad mood.

She was about to flounce out of the room when William said “I’ve got something for you.”

“What?” Her tone was completely disinterested.

“This.” He handed her a letter. “It was delivered to the wrong house. Someone’s just given it to me to pass on.”

Mitra snatched the letter with her usual bad grace. “Hmm! More stuff from immigration! I’ve got hundreds of these.”

A second later, she was screaming like a banshee. "I’ve got my leave to remain! I’m in! I don’t believe it. Look!” she thrust the letter under William’s nose. “I can do as I like now!”

Giselle and Mary crowded round her to read the news. She grabbed them both and danced them around the room.

"Don't forget you'll have to move out now and find your own accommodation." William warned.

"The law says you're nineteen, so you'll get income support."

"Well, it's my real birthday next week and I will be sixteen, not nineteen, remember."

"How could I forget? You've told me enough times. Count this as a birthday present."

"I can't believe it! This is so great!" She danced around again, kicking off her shoes and sending them flying into the air.

"There's lots of things you've got to remember." William warned. "You'll need to go to the housing office as soon as possible otherwise you'll be homeless in four weeks' time."

But Mitra wasn't listening. She was sitting on the floor in a corner, stabbing furiously at the keys on her phone.

"I'll send a text to Amir. He'll be thrilled," said Mary.

"Already done it! And Lazlo and Paul! I'm telling Vicar Rob just now! Where's Hafida? She must be in her room. I'll go and tell her."

William gave up at this point. "I'll come back in a few days, when she's calmed down a bit." He shrugged his shoulders and wrote something on his clipboard. "Anything else?"

"If there is, we've forgotten it now," Giselle answered.

"Ok, bye for now." With a quick wave of his hand he was on his way.

Hafida crept downstairs and peered cautiously round the door.

Mitra bounced in front of her. "She was waiting to come in till she heard the front door close. She didn't want to see William, but I've got her here for a celebration." She held Hafida's hand and pulled her into the room.

Then Mitra rushed out to the shops and returned later with a large tin of sweets and chocolates. "We'll open these when everybody gets here. I've told them all to come. It's taken all my money, but I'll starve till Monday. I don't care."

"That won't happen," said Mary.

“Bien sur!” Giselle added and even Hafida said, “No, I give. Don’t worry.”

There had never been such good news before. Mitra’s leave to remain gave hope to the friends. They had heard rumours of an amnesty for people who had been in the country for seven years without causing problems or breaking the law. Children at age seven who were born in the UK also had rights. But none of the housemates qualified and the laws changed so frequently that even their solicitors were not keeping up. So this was a definite reason for optimism.

Lazlo and his parents arrived soon after being summoned by Mitra, anxious to know what the fuss was about. Amir turned up a few minutes later, just as curious.

“I’ve got some very good news, that’s all, like I said in the text.”

“But what is it?” Lazlo was impatiently waiting.

“I’ll tell you when Paul and Cerise get here.”

Luckily, they came to the door as Mitra was speaking, bursting in, desperate to find out what their friend was on about. Instead of telling them, Mitra simply waved the letter in the air. The joy on everyone’s face was worth the short time she’d kept quiet. For Mitra, keeping silent was almost impossible.

The sweetie box was opened and delved into, hugs were exchanged and a few happy tears were shed. Amir offered to make a meal that evening, and of course, the others offered to bring something.

“Mum, can you make your little pies?” Lazlo asked Agneska. “Mitra loves them.”

“We’ll all do her favourite food,” promised Mary.

“It’s my birthday next week, so it will be my party, a bit early.” Mitra was loving all the attention.

It was the best day of her young life.

Chapter Seventeen

It was a long, hot car journey. Sara sat on the back seat between two middle-aged men. One slept for most of the way but the other, a large man with a fat belly, stared at her constantly. She shifted around to avoid touching him, but there was so little room she had to endure his sweaty body against hers. There was a young man in the front passenger seat. Occasionally she could see his face in the mirror. He reminded her of the attackers who raped her. She tried to shut him out by looking out of the rear window, but it was difficult to turn her head round because of the wedged in position beside the two men.

Mercifully, after two hours of this, the car stopped on a deserted road by moorland. The driver opened the doors and signalled the passengers to get out. The men gathered round a tree, fiddling with their trousers and Sara realised that this was a toilet stop. She crouched down behind a bush, keeping the others in sight through the leaves. When they started to walk towards the car, she ran after them, terrified of being left in this lonely place. As she was the last person to get in, at least her seat was now by the rear door so she could look out. She tried to concentrate on the scenery to keep her bad memories at bay.

They drove through a mountain pass with fertile fields. She gazed at the view for at least another two hours. Then the car stopped again near a farm and the two men in the back got out. She watched them making their way to a farmhouse, about half a mile away.

The ride was much more comfortable now she had the back seat all to herself. She even managed to eat the maize cakes in her satchel and then fall into an uneasy doze. When she opened her eyes again they were driving through a built up area she vaguely recognised. Then her heart skipped a beat. They were approaching the airport. She'd never been on a plane, but the old house of her grandmother's was near here, and she'd often walked this way with her.

A hundred metres further on, a woman waved to the driver, who stopped and signalled to Sara to get out. Cautiously, she stepped on to the pavement, her eyes fixed to the youth in the front passenger seat. But he stayed where he was. The driver set off again without a backward glance.

The woman took her arm and led her to a smelly toilet cubicle made of corrugated iron, by the roadside. Once they were both in there she produced a small pile of passports. She studied each one carefully and eventually chose one. Sara could see the photograph. It was of a much younger child, and looked vaguely like herself at that age. The woman wrapped up the remaining passports in a cloth and hid them behind the toilet.

"Your name is Kadia Nburu from now on. My name is Dina and my husband is Bernard." She walked up the road and gestured to Sara to follow her. There was a man standing a few feet further on, watching them. "That's my husband, Bernard. He's waiting to make sure someone comes to collect the rest of the passports from the toilet now I've chosen one. Then he'll join us and travel with us. You don't say anything at all unless someone asks your name or our names. OK?"

She had a strange African accent that Sara had never heard before. "Any luggage?" Without speaking, Sara pointed to her satchel and the little bag round her waist. The woman snatched them and rummaged through the contents. Then she handed them back. "Carry those on the plane. They'll search you but those silver coins are worthless here, so they won't be taken off you. Follow me."

Fear and excitement juggled with each other for first place in her emotions. This was it! She was actually going!

No one suspected a thing at the airport. The passport had a similar date of birth to her own, so no enquiries were made. Exhausted though she was, she never closed her eyes during the flight. She couldn't see the window, so she watched the other passengers for entertainment. The air hostesses brought a meal to each person, which took up some of the time. She hadn't realised it before, but she was ravenous. Nothing would ever taste as good again.

The hostesses had barely collected up the food trays when the loudspeaker told them the plane was about to land. It seemed too soon. Sara didn't know how long the journey would take, but from studying the globe in school, England looked a long way away. She was sitting between Dina and Bernard. She wished she could catch the first glimpse of her new country, but the two adults were in the way. Dina kept her in sight at all times. As they filed out of the plane and onto the tarmac, a shock awaited Sara. The warm air here was hotter than at home and there was a humidity that took her by surprise. Then she saw the sign. WELCOME TO LAGOS. Sara's heart leapt out of her body and her stomach rose to her mouth. She froze with fear. What was happening?

Dina noticed she'd stopped walking and grabbed Sara's arm. "Come on, keep up! People are going to notice and ask questions and then where will we be?"

She whispered furiously into Sara's ear as she dragged her along. "Don't you dare say a word till we're out of here."

It was almost as frightening as the raid the night before. That seemed like another life now, though it was less than twenty-four hours ago that she'd crouched in fear in her own home, clutching at Auntie Toto's hands, waiting to be captured. The false passport was stamped without question and soon they were in a taxi. It was pitch dark by now, so it was impossible for Sara to see where they were going. There was no chance of retracing her steps to the airport, and the little money she'd had was given to Toto when her aunt paid for her journey. A car ride back was out of the question. Trembling, she stayed silent, seated between Dina and Bernard. It crossed her mind that they thought she might escape. Obviously they weren't taking any chances.

At last, the taxi pulled up outside a small wooden building. Sara was bundled out of the car and into the door.

“Stop shaking, girl! It’s not that bad. You’ll get to England. You’ll have to earn the money here, working for us until you get enough for your air fare. Oh, and the money to buy the passport. We bought that for you.” She showed Sara into a tiny room with a mattress and a cupboard. “This is for you.”

Tired and unable to think about running away at that moment, Sara lay down on the mattress. Dina and Bernard were talking together. They weren’t speaking English or Shona. There was no doubt that the conversation wasn’t for her ears. But she was too exhausted to care. Almost immediately she fell asleep.

Chapter Eighteen

The atmosphere in the house changed after Mitra's news. Everyone became optimistic, and more tolerant, especially Mitra. The bursts of temper and frustration were less frequent and the others breathed a sigh of relief. Even Hafida seemed calmer, and joined in most mealtimes, continued to cook sometimes and even got used to Amir's frequent presence. Mitra put her name on the housing list, after much prompting from Mary and Giselle, who were worried that she'd have nowhere to go when her time in the house was up. It came as a shock when she announced, less than two weeks after the arrival of the letter, that she had a home to go to and everything was organised.

"How has this happened so quickly?" asked Mary. "The office will be closed for Easter from tomorrow. What did they say?"

"It's nothing to do with the office. I'm moving in with Lazlo. Otto's invited me to live with them."

"It's such a small place. Where will you sleep?" Mary was astonished.

"With Lazlo, of course. We're getting married."

Giselle entered the room at that point. "What's that? Who's getting married?" She looked from face to face, unable to believe what she'd heard.

"I am. Lazlo proposed and I said yes."

"But you're not old enough," said Giselle.

"Yes, I am. I'm nineteen on my records. "

"What about school? I thought you wanted an education," said Mary.

"I can go if I want. You don't have to be single. James the teacher said he'd try and get me into his college, remember."

"But what if you get pregnant? You can't go then. Who will look after the baby?"

"I won't. Cerise told me there's a clinic especially for teenagers that gives the pill."

At that point, Mary was speechless. This all seemed too sudden. She realised she regarded Mitra as a substitute daughter, when actually, Mitra was nothing to do with her and she had no right to tell her what to do. But she couldn't help feeling protective and maternal.

"What do Otto and Agneska think?" she asked tentatively.

"They get married very young in their community. They're ecstatic for us. I thought you might be."

"We are!" said Giselle hastily. "We're surprised, that's all."

"When is it to be? And where?" Mary realised there was no hope of a long engagement. Mitra had barely two weeks left to find accommodation. The Immigration department would then send someone else to take her room. She would be classed as homeless, offered a hostel of some sort. If this were happening to Sara, Mary would be horrified.

"We'll marry as soon as we can find a church to marry us. Lazlo's family are Catholic, otherwise I'd ask Vicar Rob. My parents are Christian, but I don't know if they're Catholic or not. I don't even know if I was christened."

"My church is very welcoming. The priest is from the Congo, though he's been here for many years. I will ask him on Sunday if he will do it. If he says yes, it will mean you must come to church for a few weeks before the wedding."

"Oh, Giselle, will you? Thank you, thank you!" Mitra threw her arms around Giselle. "I'm so happy! We'll come to church forever, before and after the wedding."

"He will expect you to learn about the religion, Mitra. But he's a very kind man with lots of patience," said Giselle.

"I've got to go and tell Lazlo we have a church! It will be great to belong to a family. I can't wait."

She rushed off, leaving Giselle and Mary totally bemused.

"They hardly know each other," sighed Mary.

"That happens at home, where I come from. But the girl's parents are often involved, making sure the boy can provide for her. At least we know that Otto and Agneska are good people."

"But she's so headstrong. She dives into everything without thinking. I can't help being worried, Giselle."

Giselle took Mary's hand. "At least she won't be far away. We can walk to Otto's in five minutes. Although it will be quiet here, bien sur."

"We don't really know Otto and Agneska. They seem nice enough but we've only met them once."

"All we can do is be here for her." Giselle's voice was calm and comforting, as always.

"I'm sorry. I'm making too much of this. I need my Sara to fuss about. At least she's safe and being looked after."

Their anxieties were allayed somewhat when Mitra arrived back in the house that evening with Lazlo, Otto and Agneska. Amir was cooking supper when they walked in.

"We wanted to congratulate the couple and to assure you that we will look after your young lady," Otto said, shaking hands all round. "She is very welcome to join our family."

"Will you eat with us?" Amir had done his usual patrol of the supermarket, looking for marked-down food. He produced a lovely meal of vegetables and grilled paneer. Giselle told them about her church and promised to take the family and Mitra the following week, which was Easter Sunday.

The meeting at the church went well. The priest was old and benevolent, and pleased to welcome new people into his flock. The church was full of daffodils and ferns to celebrate the Easter service. It was a beautiful building, with stone pillars reaching up to a domed ceiling which amplified the music perfectly. The stained glass windows sent shafts of coloured lights onto the congregation. The worshippers were multinational, which made the newcomers feel accepted and comfortable there.

"It's a lovely place to get married," said Mary as they waited after the service to talk to the priest.

"I'd get married anywhere, and so would Lazlo," Mitra replied. "But it means a lot to Otto and Agneska. I want them to like me."

Father Demi patiently explained what the preparations and the ceremony would entail. The banns were to be arranged and Mitra's discussions about the Catholic faith could begin at once. A date for the wedding was set for six weeks hence.

"It seems a bit soon." Mary was sceptical. "Don't you both need longer to think about it?"

"We've thought about it," Mitra answered.

"I want her to come and live with me," said Lazlo. "My parents will feel better if we're married. In two weeks, she'll have nowhere to live. But I have somewhere. Somewhere she can share." He put a protective arm around Mitra's shoulders. His parents looked on and smiled proudly. At that point, Mary gave up.

"Congratulations!" was all she could think of to say.

Chapter Nineteen

Sara was awakened next morning by the sound of strange voices arguing in a language she didn't understand. She felt terrified, but for a moment, she couldn't remember why. She was still wearing her school uniform. She hadn't even taken off her shoes. Slowly the memories of the day before came back to her. She looked round the little room. There was a cupboard in one corner. She opened the door. Two shapeless dresses and a head square lay in an untidy heap. At least they smelled clean. A small window gave some light but the view was of a brick wall. She tried to open the window. It was stuck. No chance of escaping through that route. She'd have to think of something else.

The talking stopped and Dina came into the room. "We get up early here. You're needed to make breakfast. Come with me, I'll show you."

Sara decided that the best thing to do for the moment was to comply. Scared though she was, she couldn't show it. She realised that Dina and Bernard would have to trust her before there was any chance of getting away. Meekly, she followed Dina to the main room, where there was a range and utensils, a table and four chairs. Another doorway led to what she assumed was the couple's bedroom.

"After we've eaten you're coming to the market with me, to help me carry the shopping," Dina told her. "That will be one of your jobs."

At least she was going outside, and maybe she could find someone to help her. It wasn't much but it was something. Sara's hopes were raised a little. They set off together through noisy streets, lined with small houses and already busy with people, dogs and traffic. The fish stall was the first port of call. Baskets were arranged round the edge of a pool and immersed in the water. The women vendors stood knee deep, behind each basket. The baskets were raised on request to show live fish inside.

After some bargaining, Dina eventually chose a healthy specimen, which was then killed and handed over. Sara couldn't understand the language spoken. Other buyers pushed their way in before they were finished, and it seemed to Sara that the languages were all different. There was a new word for the same fish from every customer. The ladies coped with this easily, shouting back if necessary to maintain order.

Another, longer walk took them to the fruit and vegetable sellers. Their wares were placed on the ground in boxes. Large red, green and yellow peppers, rosy mangoes, yams and bunches of herbs made Sara feel hungry even though she had just had breakfast. There was more haggling from Dina but eventually, some purchases were made. The heavy bag was given to Sara to carry and then off they went to buy olives and cassava from a man a few yards further on. By this time, the sun was getting warmer and Sara's arms were beginning to ache. Dina watched her continually, making sure she was always in grabbing distance. She heard several people talking in English as they shopped, and made a mental note of the people and places for future reference.

At last, they moved on from the markets and Sara recognised the road they had come from. As they turned a corner, she heard someone shout to a friend. He was speaking Shona. Not daring to turn round in case Dina noticed, she studied the street and tried to memorise the brief glimpse of the face. If she could escape, and find this person, maybe she had a chance. Someone from her own country may be more likely than anyone else, to help her.

Dina gave instructions all day, making Sara fetch and carry for her, clean the rooms and cook food. The work wasn't hard, and Sara had done plenty of chores at Auntie Toto's, so she decided to play along until an opportunity came to run way. She had nowhere to go at the moment, and didn't believe there would be any wages for the tasks. The plan was to keep Dina sweet. At least she felt safer here where no one knew her. The only time available to gather her thoughts was at night, in her tiny room. Once there, she could imagine getting to England, and being with her dear Amia.

The first few days in Lagos were tiring and confusing. The street outside the house was noisy all night. People passed by, shouting, laughing and arguing until daylight, and traffic rumbled along continuously. A bang or a loud cry usually woke her, however tired she was, and for a moment, she'd be back in the village, crouching on the floor, holding onto Auntie and waiting to be killed.

Gradually she began to get used to the din. She had no idea what Bernard and Dina did all day. Unless it was market day, the couple left after breakfast and locked the door behind them. They returned for the evening meal, which Sara prepared according to Dina's instructions. Sometimes, one would stay in while the other went out. This was better for Sara as the door was left open. The windows in the three rooms were permanently locked, so the house was stuffy by midday, with no way of clearing the air. A rusty fan was attached to the ceiling, but it made a deafening noise when switched on. Sometimes the racket had to be endured. Neither of her captors made conversation with her, although they both spoke fluent English.

Apart from the one person she overheard speaking Shona on the way home from the market, no one around her spoke her language. The loneliness sometimes overwhelmed her as she lay in her room, but she comforted herself by thinking about her escape. She had to be on the lookout for a chance, and be prepared to take it.

For that reason her grey school uniform was kept in her school satchel, along with her waistband bag containing the silver coins. She couldn't find the passport, though she searched the house for it when she was alone. She realised that Dina must keep it on her person. Sara decided that the less trouble she caused, the more relaxed the pair would become. Then she could make her move. It might be a long game, but it never occurred to her to give up.

A week went by, then two weeks, and nothing changed. Sara was still a prisoner. Visits to the market gave some interest to the day. People began to recognise and greet her when she passed by with Dina. They always spent more time at the fish pool than anywhere else. Dina would argue, first about the size of the fish, and then about the price, once she'd chosen. One of the ladies spoke English well and taught Sara a smattering of Yoruba while she was waiting, making sure Dina didn't overhear. She was young and bright, with a cheerful, mischievous face.

"You'll be able to tell what she's saying, now!" she winked when Dina wasn't looking. "My name's Adele. What's yours?"

"It's Sara." This felt good. She had a friend.

Chapter Twenty

Once the church was visited and the first banns read, the move to Otto's could commence. Mitra had very little in the way of possessions, despite two years in the house. As she was going such a short distance, her clothes and ornaments would be easily carried round by the housemates. The furniture all belonged to the landlord, so there were no heavy items. Her CD player and discs were her most precious things. The CD player came from a charity shop and most of the music was given to her at the youth club. Mary and Giselle helped with the packing. Both of them wanted to give something for Mitra to take away, so they left Mitra to finish the job and set off to find something. Together they toured round the local charity shops, looking for an unusual item that she could remember them by.

They were on the third shop when Giselle discovered a beautiful white wedding dress, tossed aside in a heap on the floor.

"How much is this?" she enquired. The shop assistant picked it up and turned it around.

"I don't think we can do anything with it. It's soiled and torn. The bride fell over." She showed them a jagged rent in the lace bodice and a muddy streak half way down the skirt. "Also, it's a size eighteen. There's a place in town where they refurbish wedding dresses and put them in a collection. They might do something with it. But it may not be worth the price of a dry clean."

It was made of satin, with a covering of lace. Tiny pearls decorated the bodice. The low neckline had white flowers round its edge. Giselle instantly fell in love with it.

The assistant saw Giselle's expression. "You can have it for a fiver. I wouldn't get much more for it at the dress agency."

"Oh, I'll take it! It's for a friend. She's very young and has no money. I'd like to do this for her. I'm sure I can repair and clean it and make it fit."

"How old is she?"

"She was sixteen last week."

The lady's face softened. She gave a sympathetic smile. "Here, you can have it for free. I'm not supposed to do that, because this is a charity shop and we need all our contributions. So don't tell anyone."

"Well, I need to buy a present," said Mary. "At least you'll make some money out of us."

"I can help there," the shop assistant answered. "In this country, it's tradition for a bride to have something old, something new, something borrowed and something blue. How about this? It ticks two boxes."

She showed Mary a gold pendant with a pale blue stone in the middle. "It's new, it was brought in this morning. An unwanted gift."

It was tasteful and classy. It would look perfect against Mitra's olive skin. Still in its original packaging, it was ideal.

"I'll take it."

"You can have it for five pounds. It's worth much more. Now all she needs is something borrowed."

"She borrows our things anyway. That's not going to be a problem," laughed Mary. "The problem is, she never gives them back!"

They left the shop full of excitement and enthusiasm.

"I only hope she likes the dress," said Giselle on the way home. "Maybe she won't. Agneska might be planning to make one for her. But I would love to do this."

There was no need to worry. Mitra was enchanted by the dress, and danced round the living room holding it against her. "I can't wait to wear it! But how will you manage to make it smaller?"

"I have done this before. But never with a wedding dress. You will have to come here for lots of fittings."

"I won't mind. I'll miss you both, so it will be great to catch up." It seemed that Mitra was growing up already.

"We'll miss you, too! Especially the noise you make!" laughed Mary, but her heart was heavy. Selfishly, she wanted a young person in the house. It compensated for her lost job, her lost pupils, and worst of all to bear, her lost daughter. Soon, they'd be together. She could be sent for. Mitra's success made it seem nearer.

Two journeys transferred Mitra's worldly goods across to Otto's house. Lazlo came on the second trip to carry the heaviest bag. The wedding dress had been put away into Giselle's room in case he caught sight of it.

After a cup of tea and some of Agneska's little pies, Mary and Giselle returned home. Mitra's room badly needed cleaning, but neither of them could face it at that moment. Instead, they got out their purchases and discussed how they would suit Mitra. When they could put it off no longer they shared the task in hand. It seemed strange to know that the room wouldn't be full of teenagers any more.

By the time William came round to inspect the property for the next tenant, all traces of Mitra had been cleared from the house. Even Hafida lent a hand with the chores following Mitra's departure. They were not told of any plans for a new tenant. Though they asked, William was noncommittal and detached, as usual.

"We never know who's sent to us till they get here, just the same as you guys. Nobody tells me anything anyway," was all the housemates could get out of him.

As if the excitement of the wedding wasn't enough, Giselle chose this time to reveal some news. "I must tell you," she began as Mary was relaxing in front of the television. "I have met a really nice man at church. I would like to bring him here and introduce him, if you agree to it."

This was a revelation. Mary hadn't suspected a thing.

"He's from the Congo, though not near my home. He's called Ivor. His wife left him when he got into trouble because of his politics. He came here a year ago, but his asylum claim was refused. He lives at the church. He is destitute now, but he's a good man."

“I would love to meet him. Is he appealing against the decision? Is anyone helping him?”

“Father Demi is writing on his behalf. There’s a petition going around among the congregation.”

“How long have you known him?” asked Mary.

“Several months. But I had to be sure he was genuine before I brought him here.”

“Bring him to eat with us one evening. He can try one of Amir’s inventive dishes.”

“He can come tonight if Hafida agrees. I know she hates having men in the house. I’ll go and warn her.”

Giselle disappeared upstairs to ask permission to invite Ivor to dinner. This gave Mary a chance to compose herself. She was completely taken by surprise. So many changes in a few short weeks!

Unlike the other Congolese men that Mary knew, Giselle’s friend was reserved and quiet. She could understand how they had formed a relationship. They were alike in nature. Once he got used to his hosts, however, Ivor showed himself to be witty, entertaining and charming. He chatted about the Congo and his humanitarian views which went against the regime, but there was no anger or self-pity in his voice. The housemates warmed to him immediately. Even Hafida liked him.

“Where do you see your future?” asked Mary after he described some brutal treatment in his country.

“I would like to go back as a politician and create a better land for my people,” he said. “But I realise that may be a lot of years ahead. For now, I just want leave to remain here, and a job. I’ll do anything. My solicitor is working very hard for me.”

“Lucky you! I’ve not heard from mine for ages. Nothing’s happened since my first visit.” Mary’s voice was calm and resigned, but underneath, she was jealous of this man, despite the tribulations he’d suffered. Someone was taking notice of him, and fighting his corner, whereas she felt that she was in a long, slow-moving queue.

Chapter Twenty-One

At first, Mary hardly noticed the difference after Mitra's departure. Giselle got on with the dress immediately and invited Mitra round for approval every day. Amir spent most of his time at the house and made a meal each week for the students learning English, who continued to turn up every Thursday afternoon. They all met up at the youth club on Friday evenings. If Rob the vicar was disappointed that the couple were marrying at someone else's church he didn't show it, and was interested in all the arrangements.

Life was filled with things to do. But she missed the short time she'd spent at the college, and she missed Sara even more than before. Looking out for Mitra gave her some parenting to do. Now, even that was gone, and would be passed on to Otto and Agneska, who were delighted to step in. But soon, she would get leave to remain and send for Sara. At least, she knew Sara was safe.

As well as introducing her friends to a man friend she'd known for months, Giselle had another surprise. She proved to be a brilliant seamstress. She cut out the stains on the skirt of the wedding dress and disguised the joined up seam with a flowing ribbon from the waist to the hem. The painstaking work of repairing the lace bodice took several hours each day, and strained her eyes so much that she had to stop by teatime. However, it looked perfect when she'd finished. After a week of careful hand sewing, all that was left to do was make it fit the bride. After numerous tryings-on, Mitra's excitement levels were being replaced by frustration, and signs of the old Mitra were appearing.

"Not again!" she exclaimed when she arrived at the house following another summons from Giselle. "I was only here yesterday!"

"It wasn't quite right," said Giselle calmly. "I've thought of a better way to do it."

Mitra gave a snort of discontent and threw herself on the settee.

"Have some patience! I want you to look perfect."

"Giselle has spent every spare minute on this dress," Mary chided her. "All you have to do is put it on."

"Mm, suppose so." Reluctantly, she got up and started to take her jeans off. "Er... sorry."

Even with a scowl on her face, Mitra looked gorgeous in the dress.

"Oh you look so beautiful!" Mary was moved to tears. The admiration pleased Mitra and dispelled the bad mood. She hugged Giselle and Mary before she left, promising to come back the next day.

"About three o'clock. I've got to sign on at immigration in the morning," Giselle called after her.

"Ok, see you at three, then." Mitra waved them goodbye with a happy smile on her face.

"You really know how to make people feel better," Mary said admiringly to Giselle as they put the sewing things away. "You've done wonders with Hafida, too. She's so much better now."

"She's never revealed her troubles. I'm sure she will one day. To be honest, I'd rather not know."

"I felt the same when I went with her to the counsellor, the first time," confessed Mary. "I felt guilty about it, but I didn't want my own memories disturbed."

"I know what you mean. But when she's ready, I will be."

"You're a good person, Giselle."

Giselle merely smiled and took the dress upstairs out of the way.

The next day, Mary and Amir returned from a walk to find Mitra standing outside the house.

"Where have you two been? I've waited ages. Giselle said three o'clock."

"Giselle should be in. She went to sign on at immigration this morning. Hafida went with her. They should be back by now."

Mitra gave a snort of annoyance as she walked into the house behind Mary and Amir. She threw herself on the settee and spread out in her usual position.

"It's not like her to forget. Her mind must be on that new man of hers. Have a cup of tea while you wait."

Mary put the kettle on and Amir switched on the television. All three settled down for a few minutes. Then Hafida came in, went straight to her corner of the living room and curled up on the carpet. The friends looked at one another in horror. This hadn't happened for weeks. Mary rushed over and knelt down beside her. "What's wrong? Please tell me." But Hafida didn't seem to understand.

"Let me try," said Mitra. She spoke a couple of sentences in Dari. Without looking up, Hafida answered, sobbing as she did so. Mitra turned to Mary and Amir, with anguish on her face.

"Giselle's in custody. She's on her way to a detention centre, then she'll be sent back to the Congo. They arrested her when she went to sign on this morning."

"Oh, no! Why now? She's been here so long!" Mary was distraught. Giselle was her first friend in England. They were all expecting their leave to remain to come at any time, now Mitra was allowed to stay. This couldn't be happening.

"Hafida thinks she's going to be next. She's been wandering round the streets, too frightened to come home in case they come for her. She's given up now." Mitra shrugged her shoulders in a gesture of helplessness. At that moment, Mary's mobile phone rang. It was Giselle.

"I have only two minutes. I have no more credit. Please contact Ivor for me. I can't get an answer. He has a solicitor. It's a friend from the church. He is helping Ivor for free. Ask him to seek advice from his friend."

"Yes, of course! I'll do it immediately! We'll get you back, I promise."

"I've got to go now." The line went dead.

"She wants us to contact Ivor," Mary told Mitra. "His friend's taking his case. He might take Giselle on. She told me yesterday that she hasn't heard from her own solicitor for months."

"Hafida get up!" Mitra tried to pull Hafida to her feet. "We're going to get her back! Get up!"

But Hafida's limp body flopped back on to the carpet as soon as Mitra let go. Mitra responded with a torrent of Farsi, but Hafida merely covered her ears and stayed where she was.

"It's just us two, then." Mitra gave a frustrated sigh. "I'll go round to the church straightaway. Coming?" She reached for her coat.

"Yes. I'm thinking about a petition," said Mary. "There were lots of them going round at the demonstration. We could ask everyone we know, as long as they're not asylum seekers."

"Come with me to see Ivor, Mary," said Mitra. She threw a blanket over Hafida. "We're going to the church, Hafida. We'll be back soon."

There was no acknowledgement from the heap on the carpet. Mary gave a backward glance as they left the room, wishing there was something she could do or say to reassure Hafida. But nothing came to mind.

When they got to the church to meet Ivor, he was devastated. At first, he couldn't understand what Mary was telling him. "I saw her yesterday! She was looking forward to getting leave to remain! I really can't believe this has happened. What has she done to deserve this?"

"We don't know. She went to register this afternoon. Hafida went with her. It was just an ordinary day. They wouldn't let her go, and now she's on her way to a detention centre. We thought you might know what to do.
"

"I wish I did! I haven't a clue! I only know that I don't want to be without her, now that I've found her."

Mary tried her best to comfort him. "There's lots of things we can do to get her back. We're hoping your solicitor might find something."

"I'll phone him straight away. He's a really good friend. I'm sure he'll help."

“Giselle had a solicitor, but she hasn’t heard from him for months. I can look for his address. It will be in the house somewhere.” Mary tried to make her voice soothing and calm. Inside, she was panicking about the loss of her friend. Life was going well until this happened. “Is there anything we can do in the meantime? What about a petition?”

Ivor brightened up a little at this suggestion. “That’s a good idea, as long as she’s here long enough to find the signatures.”

“Oh my god! How soon could they send her home?” Mary was horrified at the idea that Giselle might be gone before any plans were made.

“I think the Congo is much more unsettled than the immigration department believes. I don’t think they can get her over there at the moment,” Ivor replied. “That gives us some time.”

Father Demi appeared and wanted to hear the news. Mary explained the situation. “I can be the first person to sign a petition,” he offered. “The congregation here know her well. She’s helped many people.”

“She was organising my wedding,” said Mitra. “I can’t get married without Giselle. What about my dress? It’s not finished.”

“Let’s not worry too much. Let’s concentrate on getting her back.” Mary tried to sound consoling, but she was as concerned as the others. In Giselle’s absence she felt she needed to be the sensible one. As soon as there was a plan in place, everyone calmed down. The petition would be brought to youth club on Friday, then Father Demi’s church on Sunday, after the service.

Chapter Twenty-Two

It was a hot, humid day. Sara spent the morning cleaning the floor of the main room. It was used for every purpose except sleeping, so the floor was always soiled with mud from the street. Bernard was out.

Dina was waiting for Sara to finish her task so that they could do the shopping together when a friend came round. They spoke to each other in Yoruba for a few minutes, then Dina said, in English, "I'm going out for a while. Tell Bernard I'll be back this evening and I will need some money."

Sara nodded and carried on with her work. She heard Dina lock the door as she went out. Within a few minutes the heat in the little house was stifling. The thin cotton dress Sara was wearing was soon damp with sweat. Just as she finished cleaning, Bernard returned home. The open door gave some relief from the heat, but the smell of his body filled the room.

He sank into a chair and pulled a bottle of whisky from his pocket. "Here, have some of this. " He proffered the drink after he'd taken a couple of large mouthfuls.

"No, thanks." Sara put her cleaning things back in place.

As she walked past Bernard he grabbed her arm and pulled her towards him. "Come and sit with me." His voice was slurred. He smiled and lifted her onto his knee. "That's better, isn't it?" His tone was good humoured and coaxing. His breath smelt of alcohol and his clothes were sticking to his body with sweat. He shifted his position to accommodate her on his lap, and something fell out of his pocket without him noticing. Out of the corner of her eye, Sara saw it was a wad of banknotes. She didn't recognise what country they were from. They were white and rolled up tightly into a tube shape.

Controlling her revulsion for Bernard, she stayed on his knee. This was not a time to upset him. "Dina wanted me to tell you something. She's gone out with a friend and won't be back till this evening." She didn't mention the other part of the message.

"Just you and me, then. Perfect." With a satisfied smile on his face, he held her to him and took another swig on the whisky bottle. After a little while, Sara noticed his breathing becoming deeper and soon he was snoring. This was her chance. It had to be done carefully and slowly, but not too slowly. Her satchel was packed in her bedroom, ready for a moment like this. The front door was ajar, but open wide enough for her to wriggle out noiselessly.

His fingers on her arm loosened as she carefully slid her wrist from his grasp. Placing her feet on the ground, she rose, inch by inch until she was standing. The roll of banknotes was on the floor beside her. Gently, she bent down to pick it up. Bernard moved slightly in his sleep. Heart racing, Sara tiptoed to her room and took her bag. Then she squeezed through the gap in the doorway. She was out. She ran as fast as she could in the direction of the fish market, where her friend worked.

A warm wind blew in her face. The sound of voices, vehicles and animals assaulted her ears. Her legs moved so fast it was almost like flying. Every sensation was like something new, something she'd never experienced before. She was free! It felt wonderful! The shapeless white dress that Dina made her wear flapped round her ankles as she ran. She reached the fish pond and was delighted to find her friend Adele was there, basket in hand, selling her wares.

"Help me!" she gasped, plunging into the water. "I've escaped. I need to get out of Nigeria. I've got money. Help me!"

"It's alright! Calm down. Catch your breath." Adele took both Sara's hands. "Tell me what you want."

Hurriedly, Sara tried her best to relate the story of her arrival in Lagos and her imprisonment at Dina's. Adele wasn't at all shocked. "She comes here with a different house girl every few months. I don't know where they go, but she may sell them on. You're lucky you got away."

"I don't know anyone here except you. I heard some people speaking Shona a couple of streets away. I thought they might help me."

"I can show you where to go to get to the northern border. Maybe you could get across to Niger. What happened to your passport?"

"Dina bought one for me, but she's hidden it. I looked everywhere."

"You can't fly, then. Not unless you buy another. Even then, it's risky travelling on your own. It looks suspicious at your age if you're not with a family."

The conversation was attracting the attention of the other women. "Send her to Seemi," chipped in a large lady with a booming voice. "What about Akin?" another woman suggested. "He'll be going tomorrow week."

Just then a third person shouted, "I can see your mistress coming this way."

In a panic, Sara tried to run, but her dress dragged her back into the water, which was knee deep.

"Here, put this on." Adele grabbed a piece of material from the bank and wound a bright cotton printed sheet round Sara's body and a matching piece round her head. "Take this." She pushed a fish basket into Sara's arms. "Go over there." She pointed to the middle of the pool. Sara waded across and bent down over the basket. The water was warm and the fish swam around her feet, which were slowly sinking into the mud. Her satchel was on her back under the tight cloth, and the straps dug into her shoulders, but she stayed still, moving only her hands as if she was filling the basket. After ten minutes or so, though to Sara it seemed much longer, someone called, "She's gone," and pointed to Dina's disappearing back. She was strolling along the market, deep in conversation with a friend.

"Come on, we're going. And be quick! She might come round again!"

Hurriedly they scrambled out of the pool. Adele undid the cotton wrapper and head gear from Sara's body and threw it on the bank. Then they set off. The market was crowded. They pushed their way ahead in their wet clothes until they came to a middle-aged man selling yams and cassava from large boxes on the ground. "I'll have to leave you now. He'll take care of your problem. He speaks Shona." She hugged Sara's wet body. "Come back and see me one day. I'll still be here, in the pool."

"Thank you, thank you," was all Sara could think of to say. She watched her only friend go. Within seconds, Adele melted into the crowd, undistinguishable from all the other heads bobbing about in the market.

Sara greeted the man in Shona. "What do you want?" he asked, in Shona. His voice sounded quite brusque and bad-tempered. Sara had hoped a fellow countryman would be sympathetic.

"I'm from Harare. I was kidnapped and brought here as a house girl. I need to get to England to join my Amia and I haven't got a passport."

"That's going to cost. "

"I've got money."

"Zim dollars aren't worth having. May as well throw them away."

"They're not Zim dollars, but I'm not sure what they are. They must be naira, but they don't look like the ones Dina pays for food with." She produced the wad of notes she stole from Bernard.

"Where did you get these?"

"I found them."

"Then it's your lucky day. These are US dollars. And each one's worth a lot of money. They'll take you anywhere you want to go."

Chapter Twenty-Three

Rob welcomed Mary, Amir and the young people when they turned up at youth club the following Friday.

"I'm so glad you came to me. My congregation will support you with the petition, even though Giselle didn't worship here. They'll put their trust in me that it's a good cause, and I'll put my trust in you."

"Oh, thank you so much!" Mary was relieved as well as grateful. "Giselle was my first friend when I came to this country. I had no one else. She is the kindest, most helpful soul you could meet. She doesn't deserve this." The others nodded agreement.

"She was the one person in the world who believed me when I said I was fourteen," said Mitra. "Nobody else tried to help me until I came to your youth club and I was accepted. Then I met Mary and she treated me like a daughter. They've been like two mothers."

Mitra's short speech was so sincere and earnest that Mary felt close to tears. It had been quite an emotional time. It was so nice to find out that Mitra appreciated the support that she and Giselle had given her. But being called a mother made her yearn for Sara, whose image popped into her mind. She saw her gossiping with friends in her red school uniform, making her way home to Toto's. Mitra's good news made Mary believe they would soon be reunited in England. Giselle's disappearance had shattered that belief into shards of uncertainty.

Amir put a comforting arm round her shoulder, reading her thoughts. Rob interrupted them by saying, "What about the college? Will any of the teachers sign? It's worth asking."

Mary reminded herself that Sara was safe and happy, and made an effort to concentrate on the matter in hand. Rob's suggestion was a good one, and she felt sure that James, the teacher who had asked them into the college, would be interested, even though Giselle never went with them to the lessons. The longer the list of signatures, the harder it would be to ignore the petition.

Back at the house, Mary and Amir found Hafida curled up in her usual position on the carpet. As soon as they entered the room, she got up without greeting them and rushed upstairs.

"She's getting worse, you know," Amir remarked. "Can we do anything for her?"

"It's early days at the moment. I'd rather give her a chance to grieve in her own way. If we can get Giselle back, hopefully she'll improve."

As they lay in Mary's bed that night, Hafida's sobbing could be heard through the wall. Mary had grown so used to it that she couldn't remember the last time it woke her up. It sounded louder and harsher than she remembered and suddenly, Mary saw her mother being shot and watched her crumple on the makeshift stage as she addressed her followers. She began to weep, quietly so as not to wake Amir, but the vibrations of her body disturbed him. He didn't ask what the problem was, but simply held her until she fell asleep again.

It turned out that they knew more people than they first realised. Giselle went quietly about her business, but she didn't go unnoticed. All the churches in the area got involved, including the one which held asylum seekers' social groups but was now closed for renovations. The students at the English class on Thursdays at Mary's house spread the word around to any friends who had been taught by Giselle. Those who now had leave to remain were happy to sign. Shopkeepers and market traders remembered her as a friend they chatted with on a daily basis. Otto and Agneska sought out their community for help. Soon, they had several pages of names to support the request for Giselle's freedom from the detention centre.

"Hafida, look!" Mary kneeled down beside Hafida, who was in her usual position on the carpet. "We've got lots of people who want Giselle back! The Home Office can't ignore us now!"

Hafida turned her head and stared into Mary's eyes. Her haunted expression gave no indication that she understood a word. After a few seconds, her head sank back to the carpet.

Before this had happened, Hafida's English had improved in leaps and bounds. This was just another indication of how much she'd regressed since Giselle disappeared. Mary's aim was to persuade her to go back to the counselling sessions, but how? Mitra popped in almost every day. Perhaps she would respond to her own language.

But Mitra got no response either, even though she was much more patient than usual. In desperation Mary phoned the counsellor department, only to be told that the precious slot reserved for Hafida had been allocated to someone else when she failed to attend. A visit from William was just as unsettling.

"Giselle's room might have to go if they don't send her back soon, so if that's why Hafida's like this it could get worse. My advice is get her on tablets. I'll send the doctor round."

"Can't something be done about Giselle? Mitra's relying on her being back for the wedding. We have a petition going. We're hoping to get her back. But if you put another person in her room she could be sent anywhere when she does come out, and she might end up miles away from here."

"I'll do what I can. I'll have a word with my boss. There's quite a few spaces at the moment."

"Thank you so much! We'd hate to lose her."

"She was a nice woman. No trouble at all." Even William was on their side. "I'll keep her room open for as long as I can."

Ivor's solicitor took charge of the petition and was pleased with the massive response. Ivor helped his friend as much as he could, though he had no legal knowledge. He became the office boy, performing every task he could in the evenings, after his friend finished his paid work. The whole neighbourhood was involved. That is, everyone except Hafida, who lay on the carpet all day, barely touched the food brought to her by Mary, and sobbed most of the night.

The lady doctor, summoned by William, was sympathetic and kind, but warned that there might be a waiting list for counselling, as she'd missed appointments. She prescribed some antidepressants in the meantime.

Mary was not hopeful that she could persuade her to take them. "We've been there before. The prescription ended up in the bin."

"Give it a try. It will be a couple of weeks until there's a noticeable difference anyway."

"I was thinking the counselling may be in place by then," answered Mary.

"It's a busy service, but I'll put it down as urgent."

"Thank you, Doctor. I'm sure Hafida appreciates your help, even if she can't show it."

The doctor got up to leave. "Let me know if there's any change, either way."

Mary got the pills from the chemist. It felt like a betrayal of Hafida's rights, but there was no possibility of Hafida getting them herself. The task was then to get her to take them, knowing that she would feel no benefit at first.

Amir stayed out of the way for a few days in case his male presence upset Hafida even further. They were lonely days for Mary, leaving her with time to brood on her situation and long for the letter from the Home Office, which she now believed would never come. The house used to be so busy with Mitra and her friends playing music and she missed Giselle's calming influence. The people in the Thursday group became very unsettled when they heard the news.

"If it could happen to Giselle, it could happen to me," said one Congolese lady.

"It could be any of us." A man from Afghanistan looked anxiously around at his colleagues. "Every person here."

The room went quiet. Suddenly, no one was in the mood to learn. Mary made lunch and everyone stayed to eat, but the happy atmosphere that was usually there was missing. The students were all preparing to leave when there was a knock at the door. Mary went to answer it, dreading who she might find on the other side. Had they come to take her away as well? It was pointless to ignore it, as the housing officer had keys.

But it wasn't someone from Immigration. It was Ivor, a beaming smile on his face. "My friend has done it! He's got her out! It's a mistaken identity! She might have been in there for months without him! He's gone to pick her up himself!"

Everyone in the room began cheering and hugging each other. Mary wanted to cry. She could hardly believe it.

"We can't go now, we need to celebrate!" The Congolese lady who spoke did an impromptu dance on the spot.

"I've only got tea and coffee to offer, I'm afraid," said Mary.

"That's good! I'll have tea. Anyone else?" Ivor took the orders and disappeared into the kitchen. He reappeared with hot drinks and another bit of news.

"Mitra's wedding can go ahead. But there's going to be two, that's if she'll have me. I'm going to ask Giselle to marry me."

Chapter Twenty-Four

The man was tall thin and had a grey frizzy beard and piercing eyes under white bushy eyebrows. He seemed bad-tempered and unfriendly. However, he told her there were boats setting off from time to time in Casablanca. Sara knew she was in danger, but there was no one else she could trust and she had nowhere else to go. Even talking to this man in the market place was an enormous risk. Added to that, she had no idea where Casablanca was.

"You'll need three of those notes to get on the boat. Put them to one side. Hide the rest of it," the man said gruffly, looking away from her. "There's eyes everywhere in this market."

"Will you help me?" It was a dangerous thing to ask. Sara knew by now that no one could be trusted. Added to that, he seemed old and grumpy. But there was no other way. "I'll pay you to take me to whoever I've got to see."

"Keep your money. You've got enough, but you're going to need it." He looked around the crowded street. "You'll have to find somewhere to go, to lie low for the night. I know a place." His voice sounded cross and disinterested, belying the kindness of the words.

"Why are you helping me?"

"How do you know I'm helping?"

"You didn't take the money."

The man merely grunted as a reply, and bent down to rearrange the vegetables he was selling. Eventually, he said, tersely, "I'll show you a shelter. Wait there in it till I've finished at the market and I'll come for you."

He called anther vendor to watch his wares and started walking. Silently, Sara followed, shaking with every step. He took her to a tiny wooden building filled with boxes of yams and mangoes. There was a straw mattress in one corner, concealed by the stock of food. The elation she'd felt earlier melted away. She crouched on the mattress, suddenly feeling cold and wet. There was no window, but the ill-fitting doorframe gave some light. She started to shiver, even though she was sweating. She recognised this feeling only too well. It was now a part of her young life. It was fear. The door opened inwards, so two large boxes placed against it made a barrier in case someone tried to get in. Then there was nothing else to do but curl up in a corner and wait.

It was dark by the time the man came back. When he found the door jammed, he whispered, "Let me in. I've brought a drink for you."

Sara looked through the gap in the doorway. It was the same person. He was alone, with a steaming mug in his hand. Cautiously, she removed the crates.

"Drink the tea, Sara." He handed over the mug.

She reached to take it, then froze midway. Her hair on her scalp stood on end. "I didn't tell you my name."

The man put his other hand in his pocket and pulled out a leaflet. Silently he gave it to her. It was a picture of her grandmother with her mother and herself by her side. The caption read Enemies to the party must be found and punished. Sara stared at it, too horrified to speak.

"Take the tea." The man pushed the mug towards her. She backed away, wanting to run, but there was nowhere to go. "I won't hurt you. I was one of your grandmother's followers. I recognised you straight away."

"How do I know you won't sell me, or report me or keep me as a slave?"

"Here." He passed her another paper with his face on it and a warrant for his arrest as a member of her grandmother's political party. "That's me, John Morrow, but I call myself Albert. Satisfied now? You've learned to be very suspicious in the last few months. I don't blame you, that's a good thing."

His tone was just as irritable as before. Somewhere in the back of Sara's memory she recognised John, or as he had become, Albert. There were always lots of people at her grandmother's house, but until recently she had no idea why.

"People keep letting me down. I can't trust them."

"You've had to grow up fast. You're not the same little girl I watched, playing in her grandmother's garden." His tone was softer and the ghost of a smile passed his lips. "I'll look after you. Don't be scared. Drink your tea."

Nervously she sipped the hot drink. Her clothes were beginning to dry out and she stopped shivering. "How can I get to England? Do you know anyone? And where is Casablanca?"

"That's three questions. Which one do you want answered first?"

"The one about Casablanca. "

"You should have listened when they taught geography at school. It's on the Atlantic Ocean on the coast of Morocco. And I can answer another of your questions. I know a person who can get you to your Amia from there. It's a long way across Africa. It will take weeks and it's dangerous. But you're in danger here. Especially as you stole that money."

"I found it."

"But it wasn't lost, was it?"

"Not really, no. It slipped out of the man's pocket. The one who kidnapped me. He and his wife pretended they were taking me to England but I ended up in their house, doing all their cleaning. They said they'd pay me, but of course, they didn't."

Albert's expression was kind, for the first time. "They'll be looking for you right now. That's a lot of money. They're going to get very nasty."

"I didn't know it was a lot of money. There's only a few note, forty or fifty, at the most."

"They're not like Zim dollars. Every bill is worth the goods of half this market. I reckon the man had to share it with several other people. Those people are looking for him. So he's looking for you."

This was the worst news of her young life. What had she done? Desperation and helplessness engulfed her. Her knees buckled and she sank to the floor among the boxes of vegetables.

"It's alright. You're safe here, for the moment. But you've got to get out of Lagos before daylight. And then out of Nigeria."

"I don't know how. I only know the airport."

"You can't go there. Someone will be there already, watching for you. They know you want to go to England."

"What can I do? I'm lost in this town. The market's all I know."

Albert sighed, and his voice turned gruff and irritable again. "Hmm! I suppose I'll have to go with you."

"Would you do that for me? Why?"

He heaved another sigh. "I owe it to your grandmother. She was a great friend, and a great politician."

"To me she was just my Ambuya. I never saw her being shot. Amia did, though."

"I know. I was there. It was terrible for her, and for all of us." said Albert.

"Amia's never been the same since. She's gone all quiet. She won't let me write to her in case anyone in Zimbabwe sees the address. She thinks I'm still in the village, living with my Auntie and going to school."

"How will you find her, then?"

"She told us where she was once and advised us to delete it as soon as we'd memorised the address. Auntie made me say it over and over till I got it right. Amia's going to send for me, but I can't wait. Somebody tried to break into our house. Auntie sold everything she had to get me to England. But I ended up in Lagos."

Albert was silent for a while. He stared at his boxes of vegetables. Then, without looking up, he said, in his usual gruff tones, "I'll get you there. I have a plan. I know people in Casablanca. It's the only place I know, besides Harare and Lagos. I'll get you there. I was going in a few weeks' time, but you can't hang around that long. So I'll take you now."

"Will you? Really?" After so much ill treatment it was hard to trust another person, especially someone so cross. However, Sara had no choice. Her weeks in Lagos had been very lonely. Here was an adult who might take care of her. All she could do was hope it turned out.

"These mangoes and yams need to go in my van. Clear this shed out. Then we'll set off."

"How long will it take?"

"I don't know. It depends on the borders. We'll have to bribe the guards. At least we've got money. I'll have to buy fuel as well."

Sara did as she was told. Albert padlocked his shed and they climbed into his old van. The smell of rotting vegetables rolling round the floor overpowered the smell of the fresh ones. Once the engine started, Sara began to panic inside. For the second time she'd put her trust in a complete stranger.

She had no idea where she was going. But at least she was leaving Lagos. She didn't want to see Dina or Bernard again.

Smooth, tarmac roads soon turned to rocky, uneven surfaces. It was too dark for Sara to see where they were going, so the little van rocked and rolled about without warning. Dawn came and they were in a deserted valley, surrounded by mountains. It reminded Sara of the journey across Zimbabwe. That time, she thought she would be reunited with her mother the next day. This time, where, when and if they would meet again was simply a guessing game. Albert was on her side. He must be. He knew Ambuya. She had to trust him, anyway, as there was no one else.

Albert stopped the van in a little layby. Reaching behind him, he produced some maize cakes and mangoes. "Here. Have some breakfast. We won't stop again. We're on our way to Niger. It's a straight road from now on."

Sara realised she was hungry though she hadn't noticed before. The mangoes tasted really good.

"Albert." The tone was enquiring. "Why did you keep that picture?" She stared at him, waiting for an answer.

He didn't look up. Eventually, he said, "Why do you want to know?"

"Because that's how I was recognised in Zimbabwe. I remember having that picture taken, in Ambuya's garden, but I didn't know anything about that leaflet. Not until now."

"I wanted something to remember her by."

"Why?"

"Because I loved her. Your grandmother, I mean." His tone was soft and kind, for the first time.

"Everyone who knew her loved her." Sara didn't understand. It didn't occur to her teenage brain that old people had admirers of the opposite sex.

"I miss her. We had something in common, besides the party. We both lost our partners through illness and..." His voice trailed off as he looked up and saw complete bafflement on Sara's face.

"I just kept it, that's all. I can't explain. Finish your food." He sounded cross again. Sara gave up the discussion and soon he started the van up and they were on their way. But she didn't forget that brief conversation.

It was a long, boring, uncomfortable journey. They rarely spoke to each other except for necessary food and toilet stops. The van was slower than other vehicles at the best of times, but when they travelled through towns, progress was usually slower still. Roads were often crowded with noisy cars and wagons, which would come to a standstill every few yards. Bicycles wove in and out of the traffic. Pedestrians and occasionally, animals crossed the road in front of them and moved faster along the pavement than Albert's old van did on the road. Sara tried to sleep to pass the time. The rhythm of the engine lulled her onto an uneasy doze.

Night time was more difficult. Albert always chose a deserted road to stop for a rest before dawn. After the attack in Zimbabwe, Sara felt anxious in the dark. Every little noise reminded her of the thumping on the door of Auntie Toto's house. But Albert said they had to get out of Nigeria before they could risk hiring a room for the night. So she remained awake, listening to Albert's snores and waited for daybreak.

At last, several mornings later at about seven o'clock, they came to a border.

"This is a good time to cross, I think," said Albert. "There's only one guard. Give me one of those notes." Sara opened the plastic purse she wore round her waist under her dress. Albert took out his passport and placed a hundred dollar note on the front page as they drove to the barrier.

"My daughter." He nodded his head in Sara's direction as he showed the passport. "We're visiting relatives."

"How long are you staying?"

"A week."

There was silence as the guard scrutinised Albert's picture, then Sara's face. She could hear her own heart beating. It was so loud she was sure the guard could hear it. After what seemed like an hour to Sara, the guard handed back the passport, minus the money, and they were on their way. Sara watched the barrier getting smaller through the rear window.

"We did it," she said it softly, almost a whisper. Albert calmly carried on driving at a normal pace. "WE DID IT! We're in Niger!" She threw her arms into the air.

"Long way to go, yet. Don't get too excited." But his customary frown was gone and a smile crept around his lips.

"You're smiling! I've never seen you smile before. Doesn't it feel good?"

"Mm, suppose so." But her enthusiasm was infectious and soon he was laughing and singing as they left Nigeria behind them.

They stopped at the first opportunity. Empty tracks lined with bushes stretched in front of them for hours until a dusty, almost deserted one-storey building came onto view at the roadside. It was surrounded by scrubland. The sign outside said MEALS, PETROL, TOILETS in several languages There were no other houses in sight.

"I think we can stop here. Nobody will recognise us."

Sara didn't argue. A real toilet, hot food and there were even chairs in the yard. A wash in the small sink felt heavenly. She took off the shapeless white dress Dina had made her wear. The bottom half was stiff with dried pond water from the fish pool she'd climbed into to avoid Dina in the market. Her plastic money belt was still slightly damp at the seams so she wrapped the hundred dollar notes in a discarded plastic bag from the waste bin.

Albert was sitting at a table in the forecourt when Sara emerged from the toilet. She joined him and a meal of fried chicken, tomato rice and plantains was placed in front of them by the owner. Feeling human again, Sara relished the hot food and cleared the plate.

“We’ll find somewhere to sleep after this,” said Albert, leaning back in his chair in a rare moment of relaxation.

“I’ve got two rooms,” said the owner, who was cleaning the table. “One’s very small, but your daughter will fit in.”

“That’s wonderful,” Albert answered. “We’ve been travelling for three days. We need a rest. But we’ll have to pay with US dollars.”

The man’s eyes lit up. ”No problem!” He hurried back into the building.

“I told you American money will get you anywhere!”

Sara nodded in agreement. “Things are looking up!”

“Don’t get too excited. We’ve got a long way to go yet,” Albert warned. But Sara wasn’t listening. Everything was going to be alright from now on.

Chapter Twenty-Five

All Giselle's friends gathered at the house to welcome her on her return. She was as calm as ever, but the strain of the recent ordeal showed in the lines of her drawn face. Hafida forgot her penance that day and managed to stay downstairs even though the house was full of people. Amir did his usual trawl of the supermarkets to produce a hearty meal and all the guests brought snacks. At that point, no one asked what life was like in the detention centre, so as not to spoil that precious first day.

"What about the petition?" asked Mitra, "Shall we throw it away, or what?"

"What's this about a petition?" Giselle was surprised and pleased to find that her friends had a plan to rescue her. Mary showed her all the names they had obtained between them.

"I'm so grateful! I just didn't know that so many people wanted me back!" Giselle was near to tears.

"Of course we wanted you back!" answered Amir. "You're like family here. The kindness you showed in church and at the English classes was rewarded."

This was quite a complicated speech in English for Amir, and Mary was proud of him.

"You can finish my dress now! I couldn't get married without you!" Mitra threw her arms round Giselle's neck and hugged her tight. "This is the best day of my life!"

"You mean the best day so far!" said Lazlo. Everyone laughed.

"I think we'll keep the petition, just in case. I hope we don't need to use it. I think you're safe now, but it won't do any harm to put it in a drawer." Mary's experiences so far made her cautious.

"Well, you'll be safe once you're married," added Mitra. "They can't touch you then."

"Why would you say that?" Giselle was puzzled by what seemed a random remark, and everyone realised that Ivor had not yet mentioned marriage. There was an awkward silence. Amir came to the rescue. "Just because she's getting married, she is telling all women to do it."

The others laughed and the atmosphere became relaxed once again. Plans for Mitra's wedding took over the conversation. Ideas and offers of help flew round the room. They chattered on into the night until the guests finally left at one o'clock in the morning. Amir and Mary crawled into bed, exhausted by the day's activities. There were no sounds of sobbing from the next room. It seemed that Hafida was comforted by Giselle's return. Mary had managed to persuade her to take a tablet every now and then, but the good news of Giselle's release and the hope inspired by Mitra's plans appeared to have done far more than doctor's visits and medication.

Father Demi was happy to rearrange the dates for the wedding to give a little more time for preparations that had been put on hold. The beautiful dress was finished, the food was prepared and Otto's small house was cleared of as much furniture as possible to make way for the visitors at the reception.

There was an enclosed yard at the back, leading to a cobbled passage way which was shared by the adjacent houses and the backs of the ones in the next street. Otto charmed the other residents into allowing the passage to be used for dancing, and all the neighbours were invited. Best clothes were brought out, washed and ironed and hats were dusted off. There was no real dress code, but everyone wanted to look their best. The only thing left to do was to pray for a nice day.

The prayers were rewarded. It was the first Saturday in June. The sun streamed down on the young couple, which their elders believed was a sign that the marriage was blessed. The sixteenth birthday party for Mitra never took place because of Giselle's disappearance, so this was almost a double celebration.

Mary cried quietly during the service. Maybe one day she'd be watching Sara saying her vows in front of all their friends. She was Mitra's surrogate mother and that would continue as long as Mitra wanted it. But on days like this her own situation stared her in the face. Would she ever get her daughter back? She had to believe that, one day, she could send for her.

By the time the party began, Mary had put all negative thoughts to the back of her mind. This was Mitra and Lazlo's day. The neighbours managed to produce enough tables to put together in the passageway to make a place for everyone. Food from various countries was served as people brought contributions to the meal. Polish pastries, stuffed vine leaves, tomato rice, tilapia fish, hummus and rye bread made a tasty spread. Vicar Rob and his English flock brought chicken, trifles, fruit and scones and Amir produced his best work ever in the form of a magnificent wedding cake.

Otto made a speech, much to Lazlo's embarrassment. "I love my son so much, my only child and have some nice memories. And now I have a beautiful daughter and I am the happiest man in the world." He tried to embrace Lazlo, who endured this stiffly and awkwardly. Everyone cheered and clapped and smiled at Lazlo's discomfort. Then the furniture was cleared away, music was played by Otto's Romany friends on various stringed instruments, and the dancing began. Even the most reserved of guests joined in after a few vodkas. The steps were easy to learn. No one minded getting them wrong at first.

The party went on until the early hours. It was almost light by the time Mary, Amir and Giselle wandered home. Hafida left several hours before the rest, but had stayed in company much longer than the others expected. This wedding was what they all needed after the anxiety of the past few weeks. Sleepy, exhausted and happy, Mary tumbled into bed and slept dreamlessly until morning.

Hafida got up and prepared breakfast for Mary, Amir and Giselle, which was a rare occurrence. Her eyes looked brighter and she smiled a greeting to her housemates. "I have food for you," she told each person as they sat down.

"Thank you so much, Hafida," Giselle answered. "I am glad we are all together as I have some news. I didn't tell you before because I didn't want to take away any of the attention from Mitra."

All three looked up expectantly, prepared for the announcement of the marriage. But there was a sign of concern on Giselle's face.

"Ivor told us he was going to propose. We are all very happy for you," said Mary, confused by Giselle's manner.

"He did, and of course, I said yes. He is a lovely person. But that's not all. His solicitor friend has secured Ivor's leave to remain. He's a free man."

"That's wonderful! I am so thrilled for you!" Mary was ecstatic. "When did you know? And how could you keep it to yourself?"

"Because that's not all the news. His friend has offered him a job. He needs to start straightaway."

"What's the problem with that?" asked Amir.

"It's not around here. It's in Bristol. And he wants me to go with him. If we're married he can provide for me and his friend can help us with the law for asylum seekers. It means I'll be leaving you again, and in a few days' time."

There was a second's silence around the table. Then Mary said, "Tell Ivor congratulations. I'll miss you, but I'm really happy for you both."

Her words were sincere, but her heart was heavy. Giselle had barely settled back into the house. She'd be going and this time, not coming back. Hafida's sad expression meant that she had understood the conversation. "Good luck," was all she managed to say.

"Where will you live?" asked Mary.

"We'll have to stay in his friend's house for the moment. When Ivor gets some money we can find somewhere to rent."

"He told us he wanted to marry you, but not that he had a job," said Amir.

"He wouldn't ask me until he was sure of the job. He's trying very hard to make a life for us."

"You are so lucky! He's a really good man. There are so many bad people about." Mary couldn't help being envious, but immediately the words left her mouth, she regretted saying it in front of Amir. After all, it wasn't Amir's fault he hadn't been offered a job and a home. Somehow, it sounded like a criticism.

"One day, it will be us starting a new life." Amir smiled as he spoke, making Mary feel even more uncomfortable.

Giselle broke the silence. "I shall miss my home. I miss the warm rain, the sun, the fields of crops around my village, the dancing during festivals. This move means I may never go back to live there. But Ivor and I will be safe and I hope we can build a life without fear."

"There's bad people everywhere, from every nation. You must look out for that," Amir warned.

"I know. But we will look out for each other," Giselle replied. "I saw people being brought in to the detention centre and being dragged onto planes to be sent back to where they were treated badly. I met women who had trusted men from their own country who'd betrayed them and left them with no one to befriend them. I am so fortunate to have Ivor. I was really scared in there."

"I hope you're very happy together." Amir smiled and gave Giselle a hug. He was so nice, but Mary wished he had the drive and the passion of her mother.

Hafida's appointment for counselling came through the day before Giselle left for Bristol with Ivor. Although she had a lot to do, Giselle insisted on going along, saying it was the last useful thing she could do for the household. Hafida came back looking much calmer and was able to go to the train station to see the couple off the next morning. All their Congolese friends and fellow worshippers from church wished the couple luck and promised to keep in touch. Amir went back to his flat to collect his mail, and Hafida and Mary walked home to a suddenly empty, silent house.

Later that day, William came round to check that Giselle's room had been cleaned. "She got away, then? I wouldn't mind getting a job in Bristol. It's alright for some!" he said as he poked into corners and cupboards.

"Who's coming to live here now?" asked Mary.

"Dunno. Not that many people are coming to our neck of the woods at the moment. But I've got to have the room ready. We don't get much notice." He whistled cheerfully as he went about his task.

"Is there a selection process? Do they put people from the same countries together, or common languages together?"

"We try, but it's sometimes first come, first served. We'll place women in here, but that's as much as I can tell you. You'll have to wait and see. Any problems? No? Ok, I'll be back next week. "

He slammed the door as he went. Mary could hear his jaunty whistling as he walked down the street. Hafida curled onto her penance position on the carpet. Mary stared at the television, trying to follow a programme. There was nothing else she could think of to do.

The emptiness was short lived. Mitra turned up in the afternoon with a request. "Can you come to the college? I want to ask James, the teacher, to help me get a place in September when the new term starts. I don't want to go on my own."

"Won't Lazlo go with you? I thought he might like to join as well."

"He's going to be busy this year. His father's boss has got a contract and he's giving Lazlo a job on the site. We'll have some money and I don't need to work for a while. This is my chance."

"Alright, but why me?"

"He sees you as a friend, I think. Maybe he won't want to refuse you."

Although Mary thought it was highly unlikely that her presence would make any difference, she agreed to go along. At least it made her feel useful. "Ok, let me know when."

"Er, actually it's today. He's got a free period at three o'clock. I set off on my own, but I can't do it, not unless you come with me."

Mary thought this was typical of Mitra. Bold and bossy when things went wrong, and nervous and uncertain about a chance of success. However, she was happy to have something to do, and went off willingly, hurrying Mitra along so that they'd be on time.

James was pleased to see Mary, who remained silent while he went through the procedure of enrolling with

Mitra. "Because you have no qualifications, you'll need to pass some tests, but I can set those for you. Normally, places are allocated already. But I may be able to fit you in if someone cancels. It's rare that we don't have a couple of vacancies by September. I can't promise, but if your tests show the right level, I'll see what I can do."

Mary spoke for the first time. "I can help with the coaching. Mitra is very eager to learn."

"Would you? That's great!" Mitra was back to her old confident self.

"I was going to suggest that," said James. "Actually, I have another request. Is there any chance you could do some voluntary work here at the college? Are you allowed by the government?"

Mary tried to keep calm, but inside, she was elated. There was nothing she'd like more. "We are allowed to do voluntary work as asylum seekers, but most people don't want us because we are moved on so often. But I've been in this area for over a year now."

"Good. At the beginning of the new term I'll give you a job. It will involve a police check but we'll arrange that with you."

Mary could hardly believe her luck. Mitra was right to ask for support. Now she had something to look forward to. But there was another matter to attend to before Mitra even thought about going to college. "We'll have to change your date of birth to the real one, otherwise, you'll be too old. We'll call at the Legal Aid drop in. We may have to queue but it's worth it." She hugged Mitra, who was bursting with excitement. Mary felt filled with optimism. Unexpectedly, it had turned out to be a very good day.

Amir came round the following evening carrying a bag full of store-baked loaves from the local supermarket.

"They're so used to me now that they wait for me with a little pile," he said proudly.

"You've forgotten that everyone's moved out," Mary reminded him. "Hafida might manage one piece, but what's going to happen to the rest?"

"At least we'll eat some of it. It would be thrown away if I didn't take it." He produced his home-made hummus, which he'd perfected in the last few months. Mary put the kettle on. There was a knock on the door. Amir opened it and Mary turned around to find Mitra, Lazlo, Paul and Cerise, all laughing and talking over each other.

"What perfect timing!" said Mary. "Food's about to be served."

"Oh, great!" Mitra tore a large piece from a French baguette and dipped it into the hummus.

The others did the same and soon the house felt alive again. The bread was demolished in minutes. Mitra explained the reason for their visit between mouthfuls. "I've got my study papers! James sent them by post this morning. I've come for my first lesson."

"We'd like to learn, too! We both went to school but we can't go to college until we get leave to remain." Cerise's eager face looked expectantly at Mary, who was thrilled to be asked to do something she loved. Also, it would benefit Mitra to have classmates to bounce ideas off.

Buoyant as they were, Mary succeeded in calming them down enough to do two hours of the curriculum sent by James. They went home with written work to complete before the next lesson, scheduled in two days' time, to give Lazlo chance to fit it in around his job.

"You are a lovely teacher," said Amir as they cleared up the mess left by the teenagers.

Mary smiled contentedly. "I'm so happy to be asked. Yesterday, this house seemed so empty. Now I have a purpose again. And James asked me to do some voluntary work at the college when they open in September. Things are getting better. Perhaps I'll get my leave to remain soon, and then I can send for Sara."

Chapter Twenty-Six

The bedroom was only a few inches bigger than the van, but Sara slept all night for the first time since leaving Auntie's house. Her school uniform felt more comfortable than Dina's white dress, which she was tempted to throw into a nearby bin, but common sense prevailed at the last moment, and she washed it out and hung it from the handle of the van to dry. But, somehow, it held so many unhappy memories that she put it in the bin anyway. She emerged from the toilet wearing her school uniform,

Albert was sitting at the table on the forecourt, waiting for breakfast. Despite a night's sleep in a bed, he looked as grumpy as ever.

"Show me that photo again. Have you still got it?"

"It's here somewhere," Albert replied, feeling his pockets. "What do you want it for?"

"I wondered why you kept it."

"To remember your Ambuya. She was a great lady and a wonderful politician." At that moment the owner brought hot tea and maize cakes.

They ate in silence for a while, then Sara tried again. "Can't you remember her anyway? I can. It's nice to look at the photo but I'll never forget what she looks like."

"I knew her when you were a baby. We were at a meeting in someone's house, talking about human rights. It was the first time we met. Some guards were trying to break in and your father told us all to lie on the floor. Then he threw a blanket over us and ran out of the back door. They saw him and gave chase just as the front door gave way. We'd gone before they came back and they didn't know what we looked like, so we separated and went home. He saved our lives. But we never saw your father again."

"Oh how awful! What did they do to him?"

"We never found him, but your Ambuya said she wouldn't ever hide again. She was proud to stand up and show her face for what she believed in. But she died for the privilege." His gaze shifted from Sara and he stared, misty eyed, into space. "She'd made a wonderful speech, and everyone was cheering with their arms in the air, including her. Then suddenly, there was a bang and she collapsed, flung down like a rag doll. No cries of agony, no movement, no last words. She was gone. At least she didn't suffer."

Realisation dawned. Sara said, almost accusingly "You're looking at her now, in your mind, I can tell. You were in love with her."

"Yes."

"I didn't know old people had romances, especially not grandmothers."

Albert gave a sad smile. "I'm sure we're not the only ones. Anyway, let's get on the road. There's many more miles in front of us."

"Well, I'd like to know more."

"There is no more, Sara. We buried her in secret the next day. She's at peace now, in someone's garden."

"Tell me about my father."

"He was a brave man, a great man. He believed in equal rights for everyone, male or female, rich or poor. He died to save us. At least, we think he's dead. We'll never know."

"Aunty Toto said he was a hero. He was her baby brother. She's so proud of him."

"We all are. But we'd better go now. There's days of driving to do, and borders to cross. I saw you throw that white dress in the bin. Get it back, you might need it."

But Sara didn't want to change the subject. "Tell me more about you and my Ambuya . I never imagined she had a boyfriend."

His face resumed its normal frown. "Some other time. You'll meet my friends in Casablanca. They were her followers in Harare. That's why they ended up there. They got the first plane out and then just kept going. Pick that dress up."

"No, I'm done with Nigeria. I'll wear this school uniform till it drops off me."

At this point Albert, unused to teenagers' stubborn ways, gave up. "My friends make cloth and sew clothes and sell them on a market in Casablanca. I'll get them to make something for you."

Albert filled up the van with petrol and they sat off again, refreshed by a short spell of normal living. Sara settled in for a long ride, hopeful that things would turn out alright after all.

Days and days of busy roads in dusty towns, deserted tracks through mountain passes, and long queues among every kind of transport made up their tedious journey to the north of Africa. A lumpy bed in a cheap hotel and hot street food were the only things to look forward to each day. The van broke down several times and Albert spent almost as much time under the bonnet as he did at the wheel. But nothing seemed as bad as being in Nigeria.

Somewhere near the border between Niger and Algeria they came upon a petrol station. The old van rattled in to a dusty forecourt. A cross looking man wearing a long robe came out of a ramshackle building to fill up the old faithful van. He didn't respond when Albert spoke English to him, so sign language had to do as communication.

They were hoping that the hundred dollar banknotes would work their magic as they had done at the border crossing. Passing the border into Niger had brought a surge of optimism to Sara's mind. However, when Albert proffered their usual payment, the man looked suspiciously at it, then pocketed it with a grunt of disapproval.

"Hey, that's some price for a tank of gas! A hundred bucks?" A man in his early twenties was sitting at a small table in a corner of the courtyard. Sara hadn't even noticed he was there until he spoke, but after one look, she was fascinated. Although his words were criticising, his manner was pleasant and relaxed. His skin was dark bronze and smooth, and his short, curly hair slightly softer and looser than Sara's. His long, lean frame only just fitted into his chair and his biceps bulged out of the sleeves of his white t shirt. After her horrendous experiences, Sara was terrified of young men. But this one was the exception. He wasn't like the boys she was used to. He looked like a benevolent black god, smiling across at them.

"Is that all you've got?" the young man asked Albert.

"No change." The owner suddenly found some English. However, he said no more, but scuttled into the building,

"I was told US dollars were the best currency, accepted anywhere, so I changed all our money." Said Albert.

"You should have asked for smaller bills. You're paying for half this joint. Where are you guys going, anyway?"

"Morocco, but our next stop is Tamanrasset, across the desert."

"I've just come from there. I travelled from Algiers with my friend."

"How was it? I must say I'm not looking forward to it." Albert confessed.

"It was an ordeal, ok, but my friend's family comes from these parts, so he's used to it. He knows the score. We're travelling through Africa, but he's gone to see old friends nearby. I'm waiting here for him. He'll be back in a couple of hours."

"We'll set off now, so can you offer any advice?" asked Albert.

"One vital piece. Don't go until morning. That place is littered with abandoned cars. If you get stuck there at night it gets very cold. Hey, for what you paid, you can stay here. He's got a room. We stayed in it last night." The man shouted something in a language Sara didn't recognise. The surly owner came out and a conversation took place. Sara was even more impressed. After a few moments, the owner retreated inside once more.

"You've got a room, now. It's not that great, but you and your daughter can have a rest before you take on the Sahara. With that hundred buck note, you sure have paid for it."

"That's very kind of you." Albert gave one of his rare smiles." What was the language you were speaking? I've heard it before."

"It's Arabic. I've learnt it while doing my job. I'm a lecturer at City College in New York. We get plenty of

Muslims in class. I've got students from all over the world."

"Do you teach geography?" asked Sara, speaking for the first time since she'd clapped eyes on this Adonis.

"No, but I can see why you assumed that. We're doing a tour of Africa, my friend and I, before we go back to work in the fall. The students are on vacation now. We plan to take in as many countries as possible, while we have the chance. Then we'll sell the truck and fly home. Next stop, Nigeria."

"You're going the opposite way to us." Said Sara, hoping she didn't sound as disappointed as she felt.

"My friend teaches geography, so he's a good mate to have on a trip. I did my homework, but he's the boss. He was born in Algeria and lived there until he was ten. I'm a science lecturer and I'm into genetics. I'm trying to find my roots."

"Your roots?" Sara was mystified.

You're too young to know about it, but someone wrote a book about his search to find out where his ancestors were from when they were captured as slaves and sold, then brought to America. He called it 'Roots.'

"Do you want to do the same?"

"I can't. I did my DNA test and found I was related to the whole goddam continent. I'm a mix of lots of countries. My grandparents and great grandparents were all born and bred in Harlem and their ancestors have been forgotten, somehow. They must have moved up from the plantations in the south, where they worked as slaves. They must have inter-married with lots of different people. My name's Shepherd. It's a slave master's name."

"What's your first name?"

"I'm Harvey. Harvey Shepherd. You?"

"Sara, from Zimbabwe."

"Wow! That's some trip!" He looked expectantly at Sara, waiting for more.

"We're going to see relatives in Casablanca." Albert said hastily. "It's the holiday of a lifetime." He said no more and there was a short, awkward silence in which all three knew they had to change the subject.

"Well, let's have dinner together. I could do with some company. My friend will be here soon and we need to set off to Nigeria."

He summoned the owner again with a torrent of Arabic, and within a few minutes, three plates of food were unceremoniously dumped on the table. Despite the reluctance and bad grace of service, the meal was delicious. Fragrant rice was mixed with nuts, dried fruit and herbs. Sara tried not to stare at Harvey. Albert led the conversation, steering it away from Zimbabwe. It was unusual to see him being so charming and entertaining.

A huge truck pulled up beside them. It had curtains at the windows and the wheels were half as tall as Albert's entire van. A young man jumped out. He was slim and athletic. Strands of long black hair escaped from the white turban wound around his head and his olive skin looked smooth and healthy.

"This is Pierre, Albert," said Harvey. "He knows everything about the Sahara."

Pierre had plenty of advice for Albert.

"Once in the desert, keep going straight. You'll see people travelling on foot. Don't stop for them. In that old thing, you might get stuck and who knows what will happen then. And when you get beyond Tamanrasset, go west, towards Morocco. Don't take the road that takes you due north, to Algiers. Go to Casablanca from this side of the mountains."

Pierre gave them a bag of food, and a large can for water.

"My friends gave me this, but we're well stocked up until the next town. There's an ice box in the Winnie, so we can store our stuff. We brought plenty with us."

The provisions were welcome, as most of the fruit and vegetables they brought with them had been eaten, bartered, or thrown away when inedible. Albert thanked them and they all said their goodbyes.

The boys jumped into their smart Winnebago and Sara and Albert waved them off. As they drove away, Sara heard Harvey say "Refugees, yeah?" and his companion reply "For sure."

They set off as soon as it was light. A few miles from the border, the road became less defined and the shrubs by the roadside disappeared, and were replaced by rocks, and then sand dunes. For a stretch of several miles, the path was barely visible, just a slight blur in an otherwise smooth surfaced landscape. Harvey's description of the abandoned vehicles was only too accurate. Cars and vans, some of them overturned, were spread across the skyline. Every time they passed one, Sara shuddered in fear at the reminder that they might end up the same way.

But Albert's face was set with determination and concentration. His eyes stayed on the road and his mind stayed on the task. The old van made disgruntled noises, but it kept going. The road reappeared and by some miracle, they were still on track. A few miles further on, the border guard barrier came into view. As they got closer, they could see lots of people crowding round and jostling with each other.

There was a lot of noise and bustling as the people clamoured to get into Niger. The official tried to maintain order, but was having difficulty in controlling the situation. This worked in their favour. Albert waved his passport out of the van window with the usual hundred dollar note inside. The man opened it and gave it a quick glance then released the barrier. Immediately there was a rush from the other side as the crowd tried to break through. Albert drove away without looking back, but Sara's eyes were fixed on the desperate souls trying to escape. From what horror she didn't know, but her own experience gave her insight into how they must feel.

The road got worse as they drove deeper into the desert. The temperature soared as the day wore on. Albert's face dripped with sweat and the tattered t shirt he was wearing changed colour. But still he drove on, grim resolution in his expression. Sara didn't dare speak to him while he was in this mood. Occasionally he would gruffly order her to drink some water, but apart from that, they remained silent.

As predicted, groups of between twenty and forty people were spotted, crossing the desert on foot. Albert didn't acknowledge their presence, except to put his foot on the gas until the old vehicle screamed in disapproval.

The sun went down, and the temperature fell rapidly. Shivering, they soldiered on through the darkness until at last they passed a sign saying 'Tamanrasset'. It was past midnight, so a pathway surrounded by buildings had to do as a hotel, and the van floor with a covering of an old blanket, was their bed. In the morning they discovered they were in a driveway of some official compound, but somehow, they managed to get away without being challenged.

Breakfast was a packet of American cookies and a carton of sterilised milk. Because of the kindness shown by the gift, it tasted good. Albert filled up at the nearest fuel station, paying with one of the rapidly diminishing banknotes. This time, he was given fifty dollars as change. Whether this was a good price or not, neither of them had any idea, but Albert put the money in his pocket, ready for the next petrol stop. Then they set off again, into the desert.

After hours and hours of looking at sand dunes, the terrain became full of gravel and rocks. Massive mountains peered down at them from both sides of a steep pass. The weather was cooler during the day and slightly warmer at night. They slept in the van and never saw another vehicle. Her previous experience made Sara realise how dangerous this was, but Albert, in a rare moment of tenderness, talked her to sleep with stories about her beloved Ambuya. Making conversation was a great effort for him, so this was something to take her mind off her fears.

Then, one day, Sara was sleeping in the passenger seat of the van, half aware of the bumps in the uneven road, when suddenly, they stopped. She awoke with a start as Albert switched off the engine. She looked out of the window to see that they were surrounded by lots of other vehicles. It took a minute or two for her to realise they were on a car park.

"Why have we stopped here?" She struggled to sit upright, rubbing her eyes.

"We're in Morocco, Sara. This is Casablanca."

Chapter Twenty-Seven

The students made Mary's world a pleasant one. She was doing what she loved and what she was good at. The adult students were keener and more grateful, but teenagers were the challenge she loved, and the company she most enjoyed. She had Amir, and, because of Giselle's successful outcome, she had hope. One day, Sara would be sent for and they'd all live happily ever after.

Amir was more than willing to help, checking the homework by reading the answer book, looking up difficult words in the dictionary and of course, by providing cheap meals. Mary realised, as she watched him join in the lessons, how much he'd learned in the past year. When they met his English was halting and poor. At the moment, he was fluent enough to pick up knowledge of several subjects in English, just by helping the young people. His shyness hid his intelligence. Mary wished she could read those books he wrote in Iraq that caused him to be persecuted by the establishment. Soon, he would be competent enough to translate them for her.

It was during the second lesson that Mary asked him if he felt he could do just that. It was a long task, she knew, but it might show the immigration service that he was serious about living in England and put his case in a good light. But the main reason she asked was to be able to be closer to him by learning about his life before she knew him.

"I'd like you to read it and be able to understand why I'm here," he answered with a smile. "Perhaps we could look at it tonight. We'll have dinner at mine, for a change."

"Great idea, Amir. We'll do that. I'm glad I mentioned it."

The students trooped off to Otto's, hoping that Agneska would feed them, and Mary and Amir cooked a meal together at his flat. Afterwards they sat at the table, poring over the novel which had caused so much offence in Iraq. It was laborious work and they only got through the first three chapters before it was time for bed. Mentally exhausted, they fell asleep almost straight away.

It was light when she awoke. Amir was snoring gently and there was a peaceful, protected feeling in her mind and body. She glanced at her phone. Five a.m. Time to go back to her house. She slipped out of bed, carefully avoiding waking Amir, and went into the bathroom, closing the door as softly as she could. She was about to flush the toilet when she heard a noise. It seemed to be coming from the corridor. A man's voice was giving some terse instructions. It was well known that asylum seekers were not allowed to have people staying in their property, so Mary kept silent.

"Do we need to break in, or have you got the key off the landlord?"

The first man answered, "I've got it here. We'll come back to change the locks later."

For a moment, she was confused by what was happening, then Mary's stomach churned and rocked .She knew what this meant. In an instant, the lovely morning disappeared, to be replaced by an imagined massive clap of thunder crashing around above her. After a few seconds, she heard Amir protesting loudly. Rigid with fear, she stayed imprisoned in the bathroom, listening to the sounds of her wonderful Amir being dragged across the room and hustled out of the flat. The sounds of the lift came and went. His muffled cries as the door closed were all she had left. In five minutes, her world was shattered.

Last night's plates and mugs were still on the table. His spectacles were at his bedside and his coat hung on a hook in the doorway. He wasn't even allowed to pack. She was naked so she put on his coat and ran down the eight flights of stairs. There was a fire door to the outside which opened onto the car park. She wedged it open in time to see the van drive off. Amir's face was pressed against the back window, frightened and desperate. His staring eyes didn't notice her. Smudged footprints in the dust where he had tried to escape were the last signs of him.

For no logical reason, she ran as fast as she could, down the empty streets, following the van, not looking where she was going until it was a speck in the distance, which then disappeared. Still she ran, chest on fire, lungs bursting, heart beating in her throat. Eventually she came to a bridge for a rail track. A goods train clattered overhead, making an almost deafening noise. She stood in the arch of the bridge and screamed with what was left of her breath until her throat hurt and her voice gave out.

Exhausted, she slumped against the wall. After a few minutes, she realised her house was only a short walk away. Instead of running, she wandered slowly back. When she reached her home, for the first time she remembered her key was in the pocket of her jeans, at Amir's flat. But the back door was unlocked. Once in the house she stumbled into her room. Everything was as before. Hafida was crying in the next bedroom, through the window she could see Otto walking to work, her clean washing was folded on the bed where she'd left it the night before. Glancing down at her feet, she realised for the first time that she had no shoes on. The soles were filthy and scratched and her toes were bleeding. They were hurting. She hadn't even noticed before. Why did she run after that van? She had no idea.

She took off Amir's coat and buried her head into the rough fabric, inhaling it's smell. How could life go on now? There was nowhere to go to find him, and no one to ask for help. In five minutes, those men had destroyed her world. She closed her eyes and tried to pretend he was still beside her, but it was no use. It was over.

She stayed in bed all day, not knowing or caring if Hafida heard hcr come in or not. There were sounds coming from downstairs but she ignored them. Sooner or later, Hafida would have to be told, but Mary couldn't cope with the grief and insecurity it would create for her. Her own desolation was all she could think of.

The following morning she made herself get up, shower and dress even though there seemed no point to the activity. Hafida wasn't around, so she was spared any discussion about what had happened. A few minutes after she'd put the kettle on, there was a knock at the door. It was William, carrying a black bin bag.

"Thought you might want these," he said, dumping the bag on the floor. We cleaned out Amir's flat yesterday." She opened it to find her clothes on top, and various bits and pieces underneath which had been in Amir's flat. She tried to lift the whole thing onto the settee, but it was too heavy.

"You left your identity card and keys in the pocket of these." He held up her jeans, abandoned when she fled from the flat to chase after the van. "Good job I looked in the pocket and found them. I should have thrown Amir's stuff away, but you could keep one or two of these things, if you want."

Mary was touched by the kindness. "Thank you so much. I really appreciate it."

William shrugged in his familiar nonchalant manner. "May as well drop it off as I'm in the area." But Mary noticed there were beads of sweat on his forehead from dragging the load from his car.

"Where have they taken him? Will I ever see him again?" she asked, though she knew the answer.

"He could be on a plane right now, for all I know. Or he might have to wait at a detention centre somewhere. We don't get informed of things like that. It's on to the next person for us."

There was a sharp cry from the doorway to the stairs. Hafida was standing there, listening to the conversation with a look of horror on her face. Even William reacted to the distress.

"Immigration got him, Hafida," he said gently. "It's not likely that he'll be back."

Hafida dashed upstairs. They heard her bedroom door slam.

"I was dreading having to tell her." Mary broke down in tears as she said the words. She turned her head away and tried to compose herself. Unable to deal with this situation, William took his leave with a cheery "Goodbye! See you next week."

Once he'd gone, Mary sorted through Amir's things. The script of the play he was reading to her was among the household goods. Just one black bag to show for his time in England, but at least his thoughts and views were left behind. Someday, she promised herself, she would ask one of her adult pupils to translate the rest of it to her. Right now, it would be too painful.

Mary's little teenage tutor group came round the next afternoon for their lesson. Although she felt far from ready for teaching, she could not let them down. At least it gave her something to do. As it turned out, the young people were sympathetic and comforting, as well as shocked and dismayed themselves. Amir was well loved and had made a great contribution to their lives. He was like a family member. Mary and Amir had been almost like surrogate parents to Mitra.

The students' presence caused Mary to remember the days at the college. Amir was very reluctant to give out much information there. He'd objected to being photographed. Normally, he was very tolerant. Had the capture by immigration come from some kind of enquiry or leak from the parents of those students they spoke to? Had a student gone home and innocently given away Amir's whereabouts to an enemy from his home country? She should have listened to him. Guilt crept into Mary's heart, grappling for a place beside the other, multiple emotions she was trying to cope with. She was the one who'd dismissed his fears, mainly because she was enjoying the experience at the college so much.

Another unwanted memory sneaked past her grief. She recalled how envious she felt when Giselle's partner managed to secure her leave to remain and whisked her off to a new life. She congratulated Giselle, but couldn't keep the jealousy from her voice. She told Giselle how lucky she was, in front of Amir. But Amir wasn't a lawyer, like Ivor's friend. Why hadn't she appreciated him for what he was?

A couple of hours of teaching made her concentrate on matters other than herself, and somehow, she got through the session.

"He'll get in touch. He's bound to ring," Paul tried to reassure Mary as the friends prepared to leave.

"I know he can't," she replied. "I've got his phone. It's with his stuff, in a bin bag. They pulled him out of his home and didn't let him take anything with him. There was only one thing missing as far as I can tell. He had a white robe he wore round the house. They must have put that on him."

She began to weep softly and Cerise and Mitra rushed to comfort her. The boys made a cup of tea and gently placed it in her hand.

"We'll be back tomorrow to make sure you're alright," said Lazlo as they trooped through the front door. Mary lay on the settee, staring round the empty room, with nothing to do but wait until they came back the next day.

Chapter Twenty-Eight

They walked through narrow streets with tall archways under square white buildings. The traffic was as noisy and dangerous as every other town they'd been through in Africa. The air was warm and much less humid than Lagos and more pleasant than the desert. Sara knew they were approaching the market before it came into view. Smells of new leather mingled with a heavy scent of spices, growing stronger with every step.

"We're all market traders in my family," Albert explained as they grew near enough to see the stalls and shoppers making their way round them. "My niece and her husband sell colourful cloth and make clothes to order. They were great supporters of your grandmother. They will welcome you."

Sara couldn't help feeling apprehensive. She had no other course but to go with Albert. He was her route out of Lagos. But she'd trusted people before. Soon, however, amid stalls selling olives, clay cooking pots, handbags and vegetables, she spotted some drapes hanging from a wooden rod. They were multi-coloured. Deep reds and purples, midnight blues and golds caught her eye. This must be the place.

A young woman ran out and greeted Albert in Shona. "You made it at last! We thought you were coming by plane. We've been to the airport, looking for you."

"Well, plans changed a bit. I've brought a visitor. Sara, this is my niece, Elda. Elda, this is Sara, Oona Moya's granddaughter."

The look of amazement on Elda's face was almost comical. But she took Sara's hand and said, "Welcome to Morocco. This is my husband, Emmi."

Sara smiled politely but said nothing. How did these people know who she was? Elda noticed her confusion. "We were her followers and we believed in her. She was a wonderful leader." She smiled at the memory. "We looked up to her. When she was shot, we got as far away from Zimbabwe as possible. Every person who agreed with her ideas was in danger. We ended up here because Emmi has relatives nearby."

"We're hoping you could let her stay with you for a few days," Albert said to Elda.

"Of course! Anything we can do to help."

Emmi disappeared and returned with welcome mugs of strong coffee. Albert and Sara hung around until the market closed, and then went home with the couple. They had a small flat a short walk away, under an arch in a high, ornate white building. Elda gave Sara a nightgown and showed her the washroom outside in the yard. It was good to wash her body and clothes. She felt refreshed and wide awake for the first time since she'd left Lagos. She made her way back to join the others. As she was about to enter the room, she heard Albert's voice. He had his back to her.

"I couldn't leave her there, she was in so much danger."

"How did you find her?" Elda was out of sight of the door.

"She found me. She's a resourceful girl, and brave too. She's Oona's grandchild alright."

"How on earth did she find you, in a Lagos market, where it's so busy and crowded?"

"She'd been kidnapped and used as a house girl. Her kidnappers took her to the market to carry the shopping and she said she heard someone speaking Shona. It was probably me, on the phone to you. I'm usually shouting because the line's so bad. So when she escaped, she came looking for me."

"You came all this way by road, but you had a plane ticket."

"I couldn't leave her. She was alone and desperate. She was wearing a dress that was wet from the knees down. She'd jumped into the fish pool to avoid the kidnappers. I recognised her straightaway, but she was much thinner and malnourished since I last saw her, before Oona died. "

"You've done something incredible."

"She's worth it. She's such a courageous kid."

At this point, Elda got up and saw Sara in the doorway. Albert followed her gaze and growled, "Listening to other people's conversations?"

Despite his gruff manner, Sara ran over and hugged him. He gave a snort of disapproval, but Elda laughed and said, "He's thrilled, really," and Albert couldn't stop a smile from curling around his lips.

"Oona did so much for us," Albert explained. "I couldn't let her down."

"It was so dangerous a journey, though," said Elda.

"It's not over yet. Not for Sara, anyway. I'll stay here, but Sara wants to go to England to join Mary."

"We can get her there. Emmi knows everyone round here. I'll send him out to arrange it. Does Mary know you're coming, Sara?"

"No, she won't let us contact her until she gets leave to remain. But I memorised the address. I'll find her."

"You're a resourceful little girl," said Elda admiringly. "You'll do it."

"I'm not a little girl any more. I'm fifteen!" Sara was deeply offended. However, the others merely laughed indulgently.

Emmi went out at first light the following day and came back at noon having organised a place on a sea fishing craft which aimed to set off in a few days' time. The currents could be treacherous, so no date was given. She would have to be ready every day until she was notified that the sea was calm enough. Elda set about making food which would last for several days and Emmi made a dress for her. Sara chose the cloth, a soft cotton in ruby red and gold. It was the most beautiful dress she'd ever seen. She managed to cram the dress, some Moroccan pastries, nuts, olives and water bottles in her school bag.

After her treatment at Dina's, Sara was overwhelmed by such kindness. It reminded her of life with Aunty Toto, who had tried so hard to make her happy. That life now seemed a long time ago. So much had happened in the last weeks that school and a home was a distant memory.

When at last a text came to tell her to be at the harbour at midnight the next night, Sara was thrilled and afraid at the same time. Emmi and Elda hugged her goodbye and made her promise to get in touch when she arrived in England. Albert drove her to the harbour. Once they were alone in the van, Sara asked him something that puzzled her. "Why didn't you tell them about the money? That's why you got me away so quickly."

"You never know who's listening to conversations. Thieves are everywhere, not just in Lagos. The difference in Lagos is that someone knew you had all that money and probably was threatened and needed it back badly."

"I have some left, in my purse under my clothes." She took out two notes and put the rest back in the purse. "Will this be enough?"

"Emmi said so."

There were three one hundred dollar notes left, loosely wrapped in a plastic bag and tucked into the purse round her waist. Except for the contents of her satchel, it was all she had.

They reached the harbour. Effusive goodbyes were out of the question. They dared not attract too much attention. A man approached them, asked their names then took the two hundred dollars and told Sara to wait in the shadows. Albert waved his hand as he climbed into his van. In seconds, he was gone. Sara sat under a tree, alone in the dark and once again at the mercy of strangers.

Chapter Twenty-Nine

Mary kept herself as occupied as she could. It was a way of dealing with the loneliness she was feeling. It didn't fill the gap left by Amir, but it certainly gave her other things to concentrate on. The teenagers' class was important to her. She wanted so much to make a success of tutoring the friends so they could secure a place at college. There was no guarantee that there would be a vacancy in September but with her help, they would be ready if there was.

The adults came to learn English and Mitra always turned up with her knowledge of Farsi and Arabic so the lessons continued with a limited programme. Giselle was sorely missed by the French speakers, but somehow, Mary got them to make progress.

Concentrating on keeping busy made her less aware of Hafida's mood since Amir's disappearance. Mary spent long nights in her bed, wondering what Amir was doing, and whether he was in prison, or worse. Wrapped up in her own sorrow, she failed to notice that Hafida's sobbing went on all night sometimes. She came to the table at mealtimes if Mary called her, but if Mary went shopping, Hafida was never downstairs when she returned. So she was surprised when she returned from the supermarket one day to find Hafida curled up once again in her corner of the living room.

"Hafida, I've brought some chicken. The halal butcher had an offer on." Mary didn't really expect a response, but thought the information would be processed. Hafida didn't show any sign of acknowledgement, but Mary was hopeful that Hafida might try some. She looked even thinner than before.

Mary set about cooking a meal and soon, delicious smells of herbs and spices filled the house. She kept chatting to Hafida about things that Mitra and Lazlo had said on their last visit, to make Hafida aware that she was still in the room. She knew Hafida wouldn't join in the conversation, but it was better than ignoring her.

Once the meal was ready, Mary put a plate on the table before busying herself by checking the teenagers' homework from the previous lesson. Sometimes, Hafida couldn't bear to eat with other people but would take food to her room if she was hungry enough. But several hours later, when Mary was about to go to bed, the meal was still untouched and Hafida was still in the same position.

The next morning, Mary came down to find Hafida was curled up on the rug. She had no idea if she had been there all night, or merely got up early, but the chicken dinner was on the table just as Mary left it.

"Hafida!" she shook her gently by the shoulder. Hafida opened her eyes.

"They will take me, Mary. Like they took Amir." She closed her eyes again.

"Please, come and have some breakfast. I'll make a cup of tea. You must be thirsty."

"I must stay here. I am waiting."

Mary felt helpless. Hafida looked terrible. Her skin had a yellow tinge and her eyes were sunken. Her body was so thin it was hard to make out where it was among the folds of her gown. The only thing she could think of in this situation was to phone the doctor, but she knew it would frighten Hafida if someone else came into the house. There was a chance that the lady doctor whom she knew might be on call. Hafida would realise it wasn't the immigration officer coming to take her away.

She phoned the surgery, and by some miracle, the right doctor was on visits in the area. She arrived an hour later, and immediately took a sympathetic and understanding view of things. An interpreter was phoned, and somehow, Hafida was coaxed into talking about what she was afraid of. Some of it didn't make sense, but the gist of it was that she'd done something so wrong that she always knew she'd be punished and by some mistake, Amir had been taken instead of herself.

The kind doctor did her best to reassure her and gave her tablets and persuaded her to go to bed. She promised to return in a few hours' time, after the pills had made her sleep. But a different person turned up at teatime. Hafida was back in her position on the carpet by then, and the male doctor was at the end of a busy day.

"The other doctor said she'd call round," said Mary as she opened the door.

"She's got an emergency to deal with," he said tersely, striding into the room.

Hafida gave a cry when she heard his voice.

"She's scared of men," Mary explained. "She might not know why you're here."

The doctor didn't answer, but bent down and began to examine Hafida without an attempt to explain, while she lay curled up on the carpet. She gave a piercing scream and recoiled. The doctor then abandoned the task and got up. Muttering something inaudible, he fiddled impatiently with his phone.

He went outside to have a conversation, and came back in for long enough to say "An ambulance is coming for her. Not sure what time, they're very stretched at the moment. Take this letter." Then he hurried to his car and drove off.

It was nine at night before the ambulance came. Mary packed a carrier bag with toiletries and pyjamas to take with them. During the journey, she tried to reassure Hafida that she was not going back to Afghanistan, but only to a hospital for treatment. Hafida merely held on to her hand with both hers.

The nursing staff led her to a light, pleasant room with a bed and cupboard. Hafida looked around, terrified as the nurses tried to reassure her she was safe. Mary looked on anxiously as they talked soothingly in English without response.

"When she gets like this, she forgets all her knowledge of the language," Mary explained, "but normally, she can understand."

"We'll get an interpreter here. Don't worry, we'll look after her."

Reluctantly, Mary left them to it. Hafida's frightened eyes followed her to the ward door, and in Mary's mind, through the journey home and into the house.

The next morning, after Mary had phoned him, William came round to find out all the details.

"She was bad enough when Giselle got taken, but this business with Amir really put the frighteners on her." William was writing on his clipboard as he spoke. "Any idea what they're going to do with her?"

"They didn't tell me anything. She's going to be assessed today."

"We need to know if she's coming back. We can't keep this house without tenants. It might be useful for a family."

"What about me, then? Where will I go?"

"Don't worry, we'll get you a flat or something. It'll be sorted out, anyway."

This was not good news. Mary had no desire to move from the house, lonely though it was without the others. But worse was to come. Later that day, she visited the hospital. The nursing staff told her there were plans to move Hafida to another town where the psychiatry unit was more experienced in dealing with war victims from other countries.

"Don't worry," a kind nurse tried to reassure Mary. "Other patients and staff may be able to speak her language. Perhaps she won't feel so isolated."

"She might think she's back in Afghanistan. That's her worst fear. A friend was put in a detention centre and it terrified Hafida. It turned out to be a mistake, but she's just waiting to be next. Then another friend was taken and we have no idea what's become of him."

"She will be informed of everything we do. We'll let you know when she moves, and then you can go and see her. Seeing you will tell her she's still in England."

This conversation did little to ease Mary's fears, but there was nothing else she could say. The counsellors were the only people who knew Hafida's story. Perhaps they could help. But a visit to the counsellor's offices, which were in the same building, proved fruitless. The receptionist told her that patient's details were not allowed to be given to friends or relatives. She promised to pass on a message that Hafida was in hospital but it was then up to either the ward staff or the counsellors themselves to get in touch with each other.

William did little to allay her fears when he came round latcr that day. "If the hospital moves her from our area we can move somebody else into her room. It's the new place's responsibility then."

"Wouldn't she be better coming back to somewhere familiar when the treatment is over? That would help with her recovery, surely."

"That's not up to me. Besides, we need to fill these rooms. There's two sisters coming up from the Immigration centre in Croydon. They might be put in here."

"Hafida's room will still be empty, even if they come. There's a chance she'll be
back."

William gave his usual 'not my problem' shrug. "Just depends how long she's in there. Anyway, see you next week."

He was gone before Mary had a chance to ask more questions. The noise of the slamming of the door reverberated round the house, accentuating the silence when it stopped. Mary switched the television on. It was comforting to hear another human voice.

The next morning she woke up with an idea in her head. She would phone Giselle for some understanding and sympathy. She was always the person who could offer comfort and advice. At least she would listen.

"The lovely Amir! I can't believe it. And my poor friend Mary! All alone again! I am so sorry! Please tell me what happened."

Her soothing voice was like a warm blanket keeping out the cold for a brief respite. The whole story, including the barefoot run after the van, was recounted and relived. Giselle let her carry on without interruption. When the tale finished, she made a suggestion.

"Come to see Ivor and me. There's a bus that's very cheap. If you buy a ticket with your allowance money, we can give you food."

Now that Hafida was being looked after in hospital, there was no need to hang around the house. The tutor groups could wait for a day or so. Mary knew she would weep as soon as she saw Giselle. She didn't dare let herself focus on what was happening to Amir. Giselle must have lived through the knowledge of harm and death to loved ones, and could share the grief.

"I'll come today!" she said, grabbing a few things to take as she spoke. She had twenty pounds left until the next allowance day. Giselle sent her a website with the cheapest deals, and she found a coach setting off in two hours' time. She rang Otto, who had a bank account and he secured a place for her on line at the last minute price of seven pounds.

She didn't want to stay in the house a minute longer. A quick visit to Otto's to give him the seven pounds, and then she set off to the coach station, even though there was over an hour's wait. The presence of the other passengers, silently waiting, helped her compose herself. At least, now she had something to look forward to.

It was a very long ride. There were a few empty seats so after a couple of hours, Mary changed places just for the exercise. They passed hills, meadows and rivers she never thought existed. This was an England she knew nothing about. The bus stopped once by a building with a shop and a café. Everything was really expensive. She sneaked a cup of hot water from the coffee machine, then went back to her seat and waited for the rest of the passengers.

It was dark by the time she arrived in Bristol. Giselle and Ivor were waiting for her. When Giselle hugged her she clung on to her body and tried not to cry. It was so good to see her face. After a long walk they arrived at an old three storey house.

"We're flat seven" Giselle explained. "There's a lot if stairs to climb. It's good that you haven't brought many things to carry."

"I haven't got many things. You're confusing me with Mitra." Mary surprised herself by making such a frivolous remark.

"How are students coping without you?" asked Ivor.

"They should have had a lesson tomorrow. They'll just have to manage. I left some homework at Otto's before I got the bus."

"Ever the teacher, even in a crisis! I'm so proud of you." Ivor smiled benignly and Mary looked away, unable to cope with kindness.

The flat was on the third floor. The huge, old fashioned windows had no curtains and took up almost the whole wall of the main room. It was large and airy with a soft carpet and cream coloured walls. But Mary was surprised to see that it was completely empty of furniture. A pile of neatly folded clothes were stacked in one corner and a suitcase lay in the centre as a makeshift table. Two empty cups sat on top, and were hastily removed by Ivor when he noticed Mary staring at them.

"I'm afraid we've got nothing to sit on yet. There was a problem with my papers. I didn't get paid until today." He smiled apologetically, although it was clearly not his fault.

"Then how are you managing?" Mary asked. She had no idea that there was any hardship being endured by her friends. In her imagination they were enjoying a worry-free settled life at last.

"We get a bag of food from the church." Said Giselle. "There's always too much, so we're hoping you will take some back with you. It's important to look after yourself."

"That's very kind." Mary was finding it difficult to speak.

"There's a bed and a table and a cooker coming tomorrow. They've been donated, but we had no money for delivery so we had to wait."

"It's all sorted now." Ivor assured Mary. "My wages will be paid into my new bank account. Everything is fine."

Giselle showed her the bedroom, which contained a blow up mattress and two sleeping bags. "Someone gave us this for you." She produced a piece of thick foam and some pillows and blankets, which she made into a bed in the living room. “We knew you needed us and wanted to help. But this is all we have.”

“I am so pleased to see you! I don’t mind where I sleep. I feel better already, just to be here.”

“We can’t bring him back, but we can mourn him with you.” Said Ivor. He brought in some hot tea and a parcel of foil containing sandwiches and fruit.” We’ve only got two cups, but we have a kettle.”

Giselle listened to Mary story about Amir’s arrest, quietly nodding in sympathy, even though she had heard it all earlier in the day. She stayed by her side until it was time to sleep. The makeshift bed was surprisingly comfortable and she slept until bright sunlight flooded the room. She stayed chatting around for a while, then the friends accompanied her to the coach station.

“Our furniture is coming this afternoon, so we have to go now.” Giselle explained as they left her waiting for her bus. “Come back and see us soon.”

They seemed so happy as a couple that Mary was so envious it hurt. But she was immensely grateful to them. Discussing Amir’s disappearance somehow made it real, and not a strange nightmare, and as such, as an event that actually happened, she could try to face it. However, there’d been so many goodbyes in her life. Each one was just as painful as the last.

Chapter Thirty

Sara sat among the trees until dawn. By that time, other passengers were arriving, taking their places in the shadows, waiting to be told what to do. As the sky became clearer a boat came into view. It had a covered cabin in the middle, surrounded by a deck on all sides. Benches were fixed all around the deck, facing inwards. It reached the quay and Sara was herded onto the vessel with everyone else.

It was a tight squeeze. The traffickers fitted as many people as possible on board. Some were refused and given their money back. Although she found the whole process very scary, Sara was grateful that she got there early enough to be one of the first in the queue.

No one spoke for the first few hours after they set off. Surrounded by people, Sara was alone with her thoughts, her fears and apprehension and her excitement. This was the final part of her journey at last. It was impossible to sleep and as the day wore on, and conversations were started to relieve the boredom. Lots of different languages were used, but luckily, a boy from Nigeria of about Sara's age had fluent English. They chatted together to pass the time.

Sara told him of her misfortunes in Lagos. His name was Warrio and he'd suffered a similar experience when he ran away from a man his stepfather sent him to work for. After several months without pay, he left in the night and found work with someone else who gave him wages which he used to get to England.

"I chose England because I can speak the language," he told Sara. "My French isn't good, so I struggled in Casablanca. I learned some Arabic while I was there."

It was good to talk to him. The roller coaster ride of the past weeks came tumbling out. They shared the food they'd brought and compared notes about their treatment. But Sara didn't mention taking Bernard's money. Albert's voice was in her head, telling her that people may be listening. Three notes, tucked up in her little purse under her skirt was all that was left. She'd grown up since she left Auntie's house and knew to be wary of everyone. She had no choice but to put her life in the hands of strangers, so she had to protect herself as much as possible. However, meeting someone her own age, who shared experiences of betrayal made her feel less alone.

Night fell and the boat's movements rocked the travellers to sleep. Sara positioned herself as comfortably as possible, using her schoolbag as a pillow and her new dress as a blanket. She soon drifted off into an uneasy doze.

She awoke suddenly with an unpleasant feeling in her stomach. At first, the swaying and rolling of the boat was part of a bad dream. Then she realised where she was. The gentle current had vanished, replaced by choppy, irregular waves, made worse by a much larger vessel coming towards them. People were holding on to whatever they could and some were screaming as waves splashed onto the deck, spraying all the passengers in range. The ship's path was making deep waves, crossing the tide. The little craft swayed from side to side.

Anyone with any sort of container started baling the seawater out. A man stood up and shouted to the crew of the ship, who were watching them from the bridge and coming nearer every minute. Sara couldn't understand the language he used anyway, but the roaring of the sea and the wind almost swallowed the sound of his voice. He made frantic gestures, but suddenly, the crew on the ship disappeared inside. A man in a uniform stood alone in the ship's deck, waving the distressed people away.

A huge, angry roller swept into the little craft and almost capsized it. It tipped over with the added weight and somehow, Sara found herself in the sea. The cold water hit her body and she tried to scream, but salty water entered her mouth and nose. Warrio grabbed the dress she'd used as a blanket and flung one end into the water.

"Here! Here!" he was shouting, but she couldn't get near enough to reach it. He threw a piece of wood and she managed to clasp both hands on it. Her body was bobbing up and down with the current. She tried to swim back to Warrio and the lifeline of her dress, but her legs made no impression.

Then suddenly, the liner changed direction. It began to move away from the little boat. The current it produced pulled Sara to its side and almost dragged her underneath it. She was pushed against the ship's smooth surface when she felt something sticking out. It was a bolt, covered by a saucer shaped piece of metal. It was slippery, but she clung to it, and found another, higher up, and another, above that one.

Mustering every ounce of strength, she began to climb up the ship's body. Her shoes floated off and her hands were stiff with cold. The wind and rain stung her face, but she held on until she came to the top.

There was a wall of glass panels sealing the deck. It was too high to climb over. The end of a thick rope was hanging from the next panel. Somehow, she leaned far enough to snatch it and it took her weight. She hauled herself to the top of the glass wall and fell onto the deck. The jolt of the fall made her violently sick and she spewed salty water onto the floor. A glimmer of light coming from somewhere showed her that the rope was wound round a stout post. The other coils of it disappeared under a square trap door in the floor which seemed to be a kind of cupboard containing more of the rope. The rope was several inches thick, and prevented the door from closing.

There was a small, dark space at the back of the cupboard. Drained, cold and terrified, she crawled into it and hid among the coils of the rope. The rough material scratched her legs and her sodden clothes clung to her body like a second skin. She could hear her own heartbeats and her chest was burning. She made herself a little nest in the prickly hessian and waited for morning.

Chapter Thirty-One

Daylight came at last and people began to move around. The sky cleared and the wind and rain stopped. Through the gap in the trap door Sara could see the legs of the crew members walking around. They all wore trousers with a logo and a stripe on the side. They chatted to each other, but in a language she couldn't identify. Rigid with fear, she watched the crew pass by. No one approached her hiding place until she heard a squeaking noise, coming nearer.

From her makeshift window she saw an old wooden wheelchair. All that was visible of the occupant was a skinny pair of ankles with slippers on the feet. The large iron wheels clattered towards her. As it passed by, something dropped through the gap and rolled into the locker. It was a ball of wool. Seconds later, the horrified face of an old white man appeared at the opening. His stunned and incredulous gaze told her how her own expression must look, and they stared at each other, motionless, for what seemed like an age. Then the man put his hand out. Silently, Sara handed over the ball of wool. She heard his bones creak as he stood up. Then the squeaking of the chair began again, fading until it was out of earshot.

Cold and terrified, Sara waited to be discovered by the captain, or whichever crew member the old man spoke to. He was the only person she'd seen so far without a uniform. Hours passed without anyone coming, which made her feel more afraid every minute. Then she heard the squeaking of the wheelchair. Heart in mouth, she tried to prepare herself for whatever came next. But it passed by as before, and a plastic bag dropped into the locker as the wheelchair went on its way.

Was this a trick of some kind? Cautiously, she opened the bag. Inside was a can of cola and a packet of sandwiches.

The next day carried on without the capture she feared. Every minute made her feel more anxious. But as darkness fell, at last she heard the squeaking wheels again. She braced herself for whatever punishment was in front of her. The old man's face appeared once more in the gap. One bony hand beckoned her. Obediently she crawled out of her hidey hole. Now she'd been discovered, there was no point in resisting.

When she stood up, she could see that the wheelchair was empty. The old man gestured her to get in. Then he threw a blanket over her and set off, slowly, his old bones creaking with the effort of pushing. A few minutes later they came to a halt, and she heard a door open. When it closed again he took off the blanket. They were in his cabin.

The room turned out to be tiny, just big enough for two armchairs, a double bed and a table. There was a small, skinny old lady sitting in one of the armchairs. Sara recognised the slippers, but not the long white hair, the twinkly blue eyes and the kind smile as she held out a wrinkled hand towards her. Sara backed away warily, unsure of the couple's next move. The lady spoke a few words in a foreign language. There was silence for a moment or two, as she waited for a response. When Sara didn't reply, she tried again, in a different sounding language. Sara caught the word 'Rona' both times. The man said simply "Freidl" and pointed to himself.

Sara got up from the wheelchair, but her legs buckled underneath her and she fell to the floor. Freidl tried to help her up and together they struggled until she was back in the wheelchair. Rona staggered to a cupboard in the wall and produced a pair of pyjamas. She offered them to Sara, who shrank away. Memories of Lagos flooded back to her. Both Rona and Freidl tried to reassure her with smiles and comforting noises.

When this had no effect, the couple pored over a book and had several attempts at words that Sara could understand. At last, she heard, in English "We tell no one. You are safe here."

Sara nodded to tell them she understood. Once again, she was in a situation of dependence on total strangers who may or may not be trusted. But there was nothing else to do, and nowhere else to go. She stretched out a hand and took the pyjamas. Rona pointed to a door, behind which was a very small shower and toilet.

Stiff and sore, taking off her clothes was an ordeal Sara hadn't bargained for. There were grazes on her legs and arms where the prickly ropes had rubbed against her skin and bruises all over her body from the fall from the balcony. However, the warm water was soothing and calming. Rona opened the door to hand her a towel. She came back almost immediately with a tube of ointment. The broken skin on her legs and arms began to feel less painful when she applied the ointment to the sore places.

When Sara emerged from the shower room a bed from the two armchairs and the bedside table was made up for her. A hot drink and a slice of cake were waiting by it. Gratefully, she sank into the bed, and soon, despite her fears, she fell asleep. She hadn't closed her eyes since she fell from the boat, and exhaustion took over.

Next morning she awoke to find Rona watching over her. For a second or two, she'd no idea where she was. Startled, she sat up and stared around. Then she remembered the night before.

"We tell no one. You are safe." Rona repeated the words from the phrase book. Her movements were slow and she winced with pain, but she smiled as she brought yogurt and cereal for breakfast.

Sometime later, Freidl entered the cabin carrying a bag which contained Sara's school uniform, clean and dry. Her purse was cleaned but the plastic bag inside which once contained the last of her American dollars now had some unrecognisable purple banknotes instead.

Sara's attempts to get an explanation from the couple proved useless. They merely said "good, good," as she pointed to the purse. The coins she'd been given when she left Auntie's village a lifetime ago, were still in there.

For four long days Sara and Rona never left the cabin. The wheelchair sat motionless taking up space in the confined area. Freidl brought food at mealtimes which they shared between them. Rona spent the day knitting, but Sara couldn't recognise the garments being made. Several times when Freidl was out, there were knocks on the door and rattling of the handle, but Rona seemed unworried by this and called out calmly to the would-be visitor.

Sara longed to know what was said. She was still unsure whether she was a prisoner because they were trying to help her or kept in there for some dark reason of their own. However, the alternative was the locker on the deck. Even if she got there without a crew member spotting her, Freidl would know where to find her. They were both very kind, but how long would it last?

On the fifth morning Freidl took the cushions out of the wheelchair and locked them in the cupboard. After making Sara put on her school uniform and a pair of his trainers, he placed a cellular blanket on the latticed woodwork and beckoned Sara to sit in. Rona then perched on Sara's knee and pulled the blanket round them both. Freidl placed a pillow under Rona's head, which gave Sara some breathing space.

"We go," he explained to a mystified Sara. He tweaked the blanket a few times, then they set off. A petrified Sara could see a speck of daylight through a tiny hole. Freidl's movements were even slower than before. He grunted several times with the effort of pushing the extra weight.

Sara quickly became hot and stiff. Rona's frail body was almost weightless at first, but soon turned into a crushing burden. At one point, they were in a queue. She could see the feet of the people in front, through the hole. The wait seemed endless. Rona's sharp bones dug into her legs like blunt knives. Although she was desperate to move, she knew she must stay motionless. At last, the chair started moving again and she felt welcome fresh air.

They went inside again, and the discomfort was almost unbearable. She pursed her lips as tight as she could to stop herself from screaming. Sweat poured from her body and breathing required a massive effort.

At last the chair stopped and a door slammed behind them. Rona stood up and leaned unsteadily on the chair arm. Sara staggered to her feet and looked around. They were in a disabled toilet, like the ones in big shops and hotels in Harare.

Rona put her arms around her. "Goodbye," she said as she pointed to the door. Sara merely looked at it, afraid and confused.

"Goodbye," Rona repeated and kissed her cheek. There was nothing else to do but obey. Sara opened the door and stepped out. She was in a huge supermarket, filled with shoppers of all races and colours. She wandered among the isles for a while, trying to get her stiff legs to work properly. There were check-out tills and windows at one end, so she made her way towards them as best she could.

A large black man was standing by a doorway to the street. He was wearing a uniform. As Sara approached, he put his hand out to stop her, and her heart leaped out of her body. Was he going to arrest her? He was so tall that her eyes were in line with his massive chest. On his shirt was written 'Security store 3. Southampton.' Southampton! She was in England!

"This is the entrance. The exit's that way." He pointed to an opening by the checkouts. Heaving a sigh of relief, she looked across and saw Freidl buying cushions which he put into the chair. She watched as he set off into the street with Rona.

"Where are you going?" asked the man.

"Manchester, to see my mother." How wonderful that sentence sounded.

"Manchester! I've got friends up there. I go up a couple of times a year. I know it well."

"Can you tell me how I get there from here?"

"The train's the quickest way, but it's a long journey. It's expensive, so don't let them charge you an adult fare. Coach travel is cheaper, but it's even longer. The railway station's down that road. Follow the signs. Have a good trip."

She could hardly believe it. She was here at last, just a train ride away. Somewhere on this island was her beloved Amia.

She remembered that of course, she needed money. For the first time, she looked at the purple banknotes in her purse. Bank of England was printed across the front. Freidl had changed the dollars into English money for her. The English coins must have given him the clue.

Her sore legs somehow made it to the exit and into the street. Fresh air filled her lungs and raised her spirits even more. In the distance she saw Freidl's back bent over the wheelchair, plodding along the street. He was moving so slowly that she tried to run after him, but the cramp in her thighs wouldn't let her. She caught a brief glimpse of his and Rona's profiles as they turned a corner at a signpost pointing to the harbour. Then they were gone.

Chapter Thirty-Two

For the rest of the week, Mary searched for knowledge of Hafida's whereabouts. Never had she missed Amir and Giselle so much. They might have had some suggestions. Mitra and her family shared her concern, but couldn't come up with any ideas. She felt she'd let down Hafida when she was at her most vulnerable .She was so caught up in her own problems that she had never mentioned Hafida to Giselle or Ivor and now was consumed by guilt.

The teaching sessions for Mitra and the teenage friends and the asylum seekers were her only distraction. The morning the young people were due was allowance day, so she went to the shops to buy food for them. Cooking a meal for other people was a great pleasure and at least motivated her to eat healthily herself.

As she left the shop she heard someone hissing, "Asylum seeker! Dirty nigger!" She turned round, but the street was empty. A few strides further on, she heard raucous laughter. This time she didn't bother turning, but simply went on her way.

When she first arrived in England, she found such behaviour frightening. After a while she realised verbal abuse was simply just that, and was unlikely to lead to danger, unlike threats in Zimbabwe. But today, the words pierced the fragments of her broken heart and left her feeling restless and aimless; an alien in a place where everyone else belonged. She wandered back to her empty house to wait for Mitra and her friends to fill it.

Life seemed better when Mitra arrived with Paul and Cerise and amused them all by describing her attempts at cooking for Agneska and Otto. Soon, Mary was laughing along with them. Lazlo took two hours off work and came along later to confirm the fact that Mitra's efforts were inedible.

"They weren't that bad!" Mitra protested.

"Yes they were!" was the reply.

"Well, after this you can help me make dinner," Mary promised. "You've seen me do it enough times, I know, but today you might take notice."

The day passed all too quickly. After the teenagers went the evening stretched out, an aimless gap before bed time. The adult English students had dwindled down to two after Giselle left, but teaching them made her feel useful. They were due the next day. It was something to look forward to.

But the following day brought even more bad news. William, the housing officer paid an unexpected visit in the morning after breakfast.

"Sorry to come so early, but I need to inspect the house. We might be moving a new family in. This is the only property big enough."

"Where will I be going, then?"

William shrugged in his usual detached manner. "Well, there's nothing round here, so it may be another town."

"But I've got friends here! I've got a voluntary job to go to in September. You can't do this! What about Amir's flat?"

"Somebody's in there already. Sorry, but it's not down to me. Don't shoot the messenger."

"Where are the two sisters who were supposed to be coming?"

"Sent back to Pakistan. Well, they're in a detention centre, but they'll go as soon as there's room on a plane for them."

After he'd gone, another problem sprang to Mary's mind. When she left Zimbabwe she tried to protect Toto and Sara from being identified with her mother and herself. At home, letters were intercepted and phones were stolen when people were under suspicion. As soon as she had an address in England she phoned them, then made them both memorise it. After that she deleted the number and asked them to do the same. If she moved to a different town, how could she let them know? People in this area knew who she was. She could be found if anyone came asking for her. How would they find her in another town? It was so hard to find out Hafida's whereabouts that she harboured no illusions that information might be passed on by people in the area about her own new address. It was possible to get lost in the system.

She came to England believing that she would be able to send for Sara in a few weeks. Over a year had gone by and instead of making progress, her life seemed to be going backwards.

Mitra turned up that afternoon and between them they managed to help two Congolese ladies improve their English enough to understand a pile of letters sent to them by the immigration department. Giselle's fluent French and Lingala were sorely missed on this and many other occasions. Mitra's friends Paul and Cerise, both Congolese, were phoned several times, but didn't answer.

When the pupils left, Mary told Mitra what William had said, and admitted her fears about Sara and her aunt being unable to contact her.

"I'll be here, Mary," Mitra assured her. "Don't worry, we can keep in contact. Whoever moves in here, I'll tell them to come to me with any letters or messages for you."

"What if you move to your own house?"

"Then Lazlo's parents will do the same. We've got plans, me and Lazlo. We're going to work hard and save up and buy our own house. Then nobody can throw us out of our home. But we can stay with Otto and Agneska as long as we like."

This was comforting news for Mary. Otto's job and residence was permanent. At least there was a chance that Sara and Toto could find her if necessary. It would be years before Mitra and Lazlo could save up enough to move away.

"What am I going to do in a new place?" Mary said, almost to herself. "I was looking forward to working with James in the college, even if it was only one or two hours a week."

"Don't worry, they might send you somewhere close by, somewhere that's only a bus ride away, then you can still do it. Or you could sleep over at ours. Otto and Agneska won't mind."

"How lucky I am to have you. You've really cheered me up," Mary said gratefully.

"Aren't I clever?" Mitra replied, laughing.

For the first time, Mary was aware of how much Mitra had grown up in the year she'd known her. She was still a mixture of a forced maturity due to bad experiences and a naivety of someone who was still looking for a childhood. Was Sara having the same struggle? She hoped not. Had she protected her enough?

Her mind wandered to thoughts of Zimbabwe. In her imagination she saw Sara in her red school uniform, laughing and talking with her friends and doing her homework while Toto cooked the evening meal in the little house in the village. Mary longed for that simpler, calmer existence, now gone from her life for ever. How would Sara adjust to English culture when Mary finally got leave to remain and scnt for hcr?

Her thoughts were interrupted by a knock on the door. Mitra ran to answer it. A young Arabic looking man came in and held his hand out to Mary. "You must be Mary. I'm Abdul, a friend of Amir's. I worked with him once. We both came here from Iraq."

"I remember! He told me about the work. It turned out to be illegal and his friend got arrested. Amir was devastated. His friend went to prison."

"That friend was me. I was released last week. I'm allowed to stay in the country for the time being."

"How on earth did you find me?" Mary was amazed that he'd tracked her down.

"He had no work clothes, so I gave him an old pair of trousers to wear. This address was in the pocket when I got them back."

He handed Mary a crumpled bit of paper with her address on it. She'd been so careful to hide her whereabouts in case someone from Zimbabwe found out who she was, and here was Amir leaving her address in his pocket! Even so, it was wonderful to speak to another person who knew Amir.

"They did me a favour in prison. At least my English improved. That's the only good thing I can say for it."

"You know he's been taken back by immigration?" said Mary sadly.

"I suspected it. That's why I wanted to see you. He was betrayed in prison. Somebody gave his address in exchange for favours. They said he was a terrorist under a false name. He wasn't. I've read his works as a writer. I wanted you to know I didn't do it."

"I thought it was my fault," Mary confessed. "I was involved in a college and took him along, even though he was cautious. I felt safe in there at the time, but afterwards I wondered if the students went home to parents with connections to Iraq."

"I miss him," said Mitra. "He looked out for me. I really liked him. I should have told him. Now it's too late."

Mitra went home to study, but Abdul stayed for an hour or so, drinking tea and chatting about his family. As he was leaving, Mary remembered the play she found in Amir's belongings. "I've got some things from his flat. The housing man was kind enough to give them to me. The last play he wrote is here, in Arabic. Can you translate it for me one day?"

"How about today?"

"I don't think I'm quite ready for it at the moment."

"Well, here's my number. Let me know."

They said goodbye, promising to keep in touch.

Mary went to sleep thinking of Amir. She dreamt they were together in Zimbabwe, walking around, looking for Sara. Her own voice woke her up, shouting "Sara!" She got up with a start and looked out of the window. But the street was empty except for Otto, walking to work as usual.

Chapter Thirty-Three

It started off as an ordinary day. Once Otto was out of sight Mary got up and did the chores as she did every morning. Abdul's visit somehow made Amir closer. At least she could talk about him with somebody who knew him. It was comforting to know that other people missed him too.

She was going to make a cup of tea when there was a knock on the door. A quick glance through the window revealed William's car outside. This was unusual. It wasn't his day to visit, so Mary immediately suspected bad news. Surely they weren't moving her already.

"Relax, it's not a move!" said William as he saw Mary's distressed face. "Well, it is a move, but it's a good one."

"How can any move be good? I want to stay here."

"You've not read this, then," he handed her a letter from the doormat.

"I didn't hear that coming through. What is it?"

"Guess."

Her heart turned over and over. It couldn't be, surely. Trembling hands opened it, her mind preparing for disappointment even while she was hoping. But it was something she thought would never arrive. It was a letter from the Home Office, telling her that she had leave to remain for four years.

William studied Mary's face and beamed at her. "We got a phone call this morning asking us to transfer all your details to the housing department. You've got four weeks to find somewhere."

Shivers ran through Mary's body. This was it. She was safe at last. William gave a list of instructions. She nodded from time to time, but she didn't hear a word of it.

After he'd gone, she tried to gather her thoughts. The first thing she needed to do was to contact Sara and Toto. Sara could come over now, as Mary's dependent. Or perhaps she should sort that out before telling Sara. Or perhaps the housing should be her immediate port of call. Or maybe she should be packing. Her mind dithered from one job to another.

The day passed without one task being completed. In the end, she started gathering her things together in a corner of the living room. She imagined that she'd very few possessions in this country, but considering she'd arrived with one carrier bag, there was quite a lot of stuff. None of it had more than a sentimental value, but there were things she wanted to keep.

She went through Amir's belongings, still in the black bin bag rescued by William. His play was the most precious, but she found it hard to throw anything away. Abdul gave her no hope that Amir would be coming back, but putting his clothes in the bin seemed so final. If she gave them to a needy asylum seeker could she bear to see that person walking around in them? She folded and refolded them and relived her memories. So many people who were close to her were now gone from her life. This was a small part of Amir she could hang on to.

Eventually, she put the clothes back in the bin bags and placed them with the rest of the luggage. It would be better to go to bed and leave everything until morning, when she would be able to think more clearly.

She was about to go upstairs when there was a knock on the door. Visitors were rare at this hour, and she hesitated at first. The person knocked again and this time, Mary cautiously opened the door.

A young African woman stood on the step. She was taller than Mary. She wore a grey woollen cardigan that was matted and shrivelled. Her grey skirt was too short but baggy round her slim waist and she wore men's trainers on her feet.

The hair on Mary's neck and shoulders stood on end and her stomach turned over and over. Time froze and her brain stopped working. Then she heard a voice say "Sara" and realised it was her own. Was she dreaming? Was this someone who looked like Sara? It wasn't the same Sara she'd left behind. But she knew it was her. Was she hallucinating?

“Hallo, Amia.” The girl wrapped her arms around her mother and hugged her tight. Tears sprang to Mary’s eyes as she held Sara’s body. She could feel her ribs and her heart beat. Incredible as it seemed, she knew she was real.

Chapter Thirty-Four

For a few minutes, neither of them could speak. They sat together on the settee, holding hands and stared at each other in wonder. Eventually, Mary found her voice.

"I really can't believe my eyes. People say that, but they don't mean it. But for me, it's true. What happened? Where's your aunt Toto? Is she here?"

"No, she's still in Zimbabwe, living with a friend who wanted some help with her children."

"Why did she move from the village? You were safe there. Nobody knew who you were."

"That's what we thought, but some people did know. They knew us, but we still don't know who they are. I didn't find out until after I was attacked that there was a leaflet going round with our photo, saying we were traitors."

"Oh, my god! You were attacked?" Mary's horrified eyes fixed on her only child.

"Twice. The first time I was coming home from school. I changed school after that but it was no use. The second time they tried to batter down the door of Auntie's house."

"I thought I was protecting you by putting some distance between us. I was so wrong. I made you learn this address. I thought I'd be able to send for you within a few weeks."

Sara laughed. "Obviously, I've got a good memory."

"I'm moving in three or four weeks, though. Sooner, if they can find me somewhere. You're only just in time."

"I would have searched this country and found you. It's a small island."

Mary smiled at Sara's youthful confidence. "You've grown up a lot. You're very determined, like your Ambuya."

"That's what Albert said. He helped me because of her. He was in love with her."

"Albert? Your grandmother's friend? I know him. He was supposed to be in Morocco with his nieces and nephews."

"I met them as well, in Casablanca."

Mary was lost for words. While she was feeling sorry for herself her daughter was roaming round the world instead of leading the quiet village life she'd imagined.

"I did a bad thing, Amia," Sara confessed. "I stole some money. That what got me here to Manchester. Someone dropped a big bunch of notes. I picked them up. I thought they were like Zim dollars, and a lot of notes got you a day's food. But they weren't. They were US dollars, worth a lot of money. They got me and Albert right across Africa in his van."

"I must write and thank him. I'm free to do that now. I know where his nieces and nephews are. I know where Toto is, as well. That friend of hers has been worrying about her since before I left. I've got leave to remain now, so I can't be sent back. We can get in touch again. What's happened to your clothes? Were they once a school uniform?"

"I fell in the sea. I had a lovely dress from Casablanca, but it got left behind. Somebody tried to pull me back in the boat using it as a rope, but I couldn't reach it. These are the only clothes I've got. I climbed onto a ship in them so they were full of sea water. An old couple washed them for me."

"Who was this old couple? Did you know them already?"

"They were strangers on the boat. I don't know what they were doing there. I think they were related to one of the crew, because I never saw any other passengers."

"Where were they from? Where were they going?"

"I've no idea. I couldn't speak their language and they couldn't speak mine. They found me when I was hiding in a cupboard and looked after me. The boat stopped in England and they smuggled me ashore in a wheelchair this morning. I came straight here. It's taken me all day to find you. I met two men from New York, and they helped us as well. Albert and I were crossing the desert and they gave us food."

Poor Mary's emotions were swinging from ecstasy to consternation, from gratitude to horror, to disbelief and back to ecstasy. This had been a ridiculously long day. They chatted on until daylight. Mary told Sara all about Amir, her connections with the college, Mitra and the tutor groups and the disappearance of so many friends during the time they'd been apart.

"I really loved Amir," Mary confessed. "I'll never know what happened to him and it hurts so much."

"Albert misses my Ambuya terribly. He thinks she was wonderful. So do I, but just because she was my Ambuya, not because of her work. I didn't really know that much about it until she died."

"We did our best to keep it from you. I keep reliving the moment when she was shot. It's in my head always. But at least I've got you now. I can cope with anything. I'll contact Toto and Albert to tell them you're safe and how grateful I am."

They went to bed just as Otto was making his way down the road.

"That's one of my friends, and Mitra's father-in -law. I used to watch him every morning going to work. I didn't know him then. I wondered who he was and what his life was like. Now I've met him and he's really nice."

But Sara had fallen fast asleep as soon as she lay down and didn't hear a word. Mary lay beside her, watching her sleep just as she had done when she was a baby. Her mind went over the massive list of things to do when she got up. For a start, guests weren't allowed to sleep in asylum seeker houses, and William would be in and out several times before she moved. They'd been apart so long that Mary couldn't bear for them to be in different houses. She'd have to hide her.

The local housing office might offer something. William told her to go as soon as possible. The immigration department needed to be informed of Sara's arrival into the country. Sometimes that took all day. She hadn't even finished the packing. Mitra's family and the college would be thrilled to hear her fantastic news so she should go and see them. But there was one thing which would take priority. She must ring Amir's friend Abdul, and make a date for him to come over and read Amir's play. It was all she had left of him but it was something. And she was ready to hear it now.

About the author

Chetty Mobola Christina Reis. Despite the author's first names being Nigerian she has never been to Africa. Born and brought up in Stockport, Greater Manchester, with her white grandmother and mixed-race mother, she knew no other black families and was the only black child in her school.

She has always used stories and poetry as an escape and wrote her first novel aged fifteen. Although she has continued to write ever since, only recently has she shared her work.

The author began her nurse training on her eighteenth birthday before becoming a nurse, a midwife and then a health visitor. She spent her sabbatical leave in India where she taught midwifery to student nurses in a hospital in a crowded inner-city neighbourhood of Chennai.

After taking semiretirement from her post as a health advisor for asylum seekers and travellers, she joined the Society of Medical Writers where her articles, short stories and poems regularly won prizes, many being published in the society's biannual magazine, The Writer. In 2011, she was awarded the Society's Wilfred Hopkins Prize for Creative Writing.

Christina is still involved, on a voluntary basis, with the asylum seekers in her area and, as a result, has many friends from all corners of the world.

Her research into the life and conditions of poverty-stricken families in industrial Manchester in the early nineteenth century, together with stories of her grandmother's harsh childhood, resulted in a play which was commended in a competition.

The author brought up five children as a single parent, so writing became a luxury retreat, for many years, to offset a stressful job and sometimes an equally stressful home life. Now, able to choose her leisure activities, she finds that still enjoys creating the written word just as much.

As well as No Relation, she has completed So This is England and is currently writing her third novel, Relative Strangers.

Christina's poems have been included in several anthologies, and, for the Society of Medical Writers, she co-edited and contributed to Poets on Prescription, a collection of poems inspired by the experiences of health care workers.

Lightning Source UK Ltd.
Milton Keynes UK
UKHW011338290722
406569UK00001B/27